MOMMY'S BOY

FIONA HOLLOWAY

BLACK SWAN
DIGITAL

First published in 2025
Concept created by Black Swan Digital. Developed by Mark Coleman.

PROLOGUE

I wake to the sound of the wind howling through the cracks in the old lodge, and rattling the windows like skeletal fingers scratching at the glass. The pines outside groan, bending and swaying, trying to whisper their secrets and warnings to me. Only, I don't want to know what they're saying.

The room is dark except for a silver square of moonlight that cuts across the floorboards, spilling up the side of my bed. I clutch my rag doll tighter, pressing its matted yarn hair against my cheek. The stuffing has gone flat in its belly where I've squeezed it, but I can still feel the shape of its button eye where it digs into my palm. I tell myself not to listen. If I squeeze the doll tight enough, and bury my face deep enough in the quilt, maybe I won't be able to hear her. But I always hear her.

Mama's voice slices through the house, thin and sharp, like the scream of a wounded bird. It rises up from the lower floor, echoing against the wood-paneled walls of Drummond Lodge. She isn't calling for me, though. She never calls for me. But I know her ragged, desperate voice. She's calling for him.

I slide lower in the bed until the covers nearly swallow me. My lips form a single word, though the sound barely escapes.

"Mama?"

The house answers my half-uttered call with silence. Then the silence is broken by another sound. Heavy boots on hollow, rugless floors. Each step shakes the old floorboards like the beating of a giant heart. I know that rhythm better than the lullabies Mama used to sing. It's slower and heavier, and it always means the same thing. He's coming.

The boots stop outside my door. I squeeze my doll so hard my fingers ache. SLAM. It's the sound of another door. Not mine. Somewhere further down the hall. The slam makes the walls shudder, and dust falls like ashes from the ceiling beams. I strain, but I hear nothing. No more boots. No more of Mama's voice. Only the wind clawing at the house, and a wolf howling far off in the forest.

I force myself to peek above the blanket, just for a second. My breath immediately fogs in the icy air. The moonlight shifts on the wall, carving scary shapes that crawl and stretch across the room. My eyes burn, but I don't blink. I'm waiting for the inevitable. Which, inevitably, happens.

A creak, followed by the groan of the door easing open, so slowly it sounds like the house itself is in pain. The light from the hallway spills in, pale and cold and a tall, broad shape fills it. A shadow stretched long and crooked.

He doesn't move at first. He just stands there, blocking out the light, like a dark tower in my doorway. My throat locks up, and I dive under the quilt, pulling it over my head until all I can see is the scratchy weave of the fabric and the faint outline of my doll's face.

The boards groan again. He's inside now. I count. That's what I do when I'm scared. One, two, three... each number a tiny prayer. His footsteps cross the floor, slow, deliberate, coming ever closer. He carries the smell of smoke and iron, hard and bitter, just like him. The footsteps stop right beside the bed. I don't move. I don't even breathe. I press my eyes tightly shut, hoping that if I stay still enough, I'll just disappear. Or he will.

A long moment passes, then the footsteps retreat and the door clicks shut. But I don't dare come out yet. Even after the door closes with a solid clunk, and the wind swallows everything again. I keep my eyes closed, and pray for sleep.

But the house is restless tonight. It doesn't let me sleep. I hear Mama again. Only this time it isn't just her voice, it's her body. The thud of her feet pounding against the stairs, the frantic slam of a door below. She's running again. She's always running. But she never makes it far.

I creep from the bed, doll clutched to my chest, and tiptoe to the window. The glass is cold enough to shock my fingertips as I press against it. The moon is fat and white, draped in thin clouds, and the trees below sway like an army of shadows. Mama bursts out into the snow, her nightgown flapping around her painfully thin body. The wind whips her dark hair into her face, but I can still see her eyes, wide and wild. Her breath trails behind her in frantic clouds.

And then I see him follow her out into the night. His tall, terrible shadow stretches across the white ground, longer than any man should cast. He doesn't hurry because doesn't have to. He knows she won't get away.

"Mama," I whisper against the glass, but she can't hear me, and even if she could, she wouldn't listen.

She stumbles, her bare feet sinking into the drifts. She falls once, twice, clawing at the snow like it's quicksand. He reaches her easily. One long stride followed by another, and his hand, black against the white snow, snaps around her wrist and yanks her back.

She screams then. Not words, just the raw, animal sound of a broken woman. The trees catch her scream and throw it back, echoing until it feels like the whole forest is screaming with her. He drags her across the snow, with her legs kicking, and her fingers tearing at the ground. The moonlight glints off the frost clinging to her gown, turning it silver. She looks like a ghost already.

My breath fogs the glass, and I wipe it with my sleeve, but my hands are shaking too hard to see clearly. He pulls her toward the dark edge of the woods, away from the house, away from me. She twists in his grip, clawing at him, her voice shrill and desperate.

"Please," she cries, though I can't hear the words, only the shape of her mouth forming them.

He doesn't answer. He never does. Behind them, another shadow stirs. A small boy is peeking out from the porch, his face pale in the moonlight, and his eyes hollow. My brother, Stuart. He doesn't move to help her. He just stands there, watching as if his feet are nailed to the wood, and the scene before him is a television drama.

I want to scream and pound on the glass, to shatter it, to run out there and drag her back. But my body won't obey and my voice is gone. The doll dangles uselessly from my fist as I watch him pull her into the trees. The branches close around them like a cage. Her scream rips once more through the night, and then there's nothing but the wind and the endless groan of the forest. The snow where she fell glows faintly in the moonlight, scarred with dark streaks that look like ink spilled across white paper.

Stuart finally turns his head. His eyes find mine, up in the window and I see in them a glimmer of that same, cruel, darkness. I sink down to the floor, curling into myself, and pull the quilt over my head. I press my face against the doll until the button digs into my skin. I whisper Mama's name over and over, but the cold night steals it away. Somewhere in the house, the door slams again. His boots thunder on the floorboards. I close my eyes and pray to vanish into the dark. Because I know what comes next.

1

The whole room feels like it was designed to remind me I don't belong here. The chandeliers glow above me in dripping tiers, heavy with crystal that scatters the light across the polished floor. The wood panels on the walls gleam so richly they almost reflect the faces drifting by, powdered and preened in a way that I can never be. The Boston Athenaeum, with its marble busts and velvet drapery, has been a library for centuries, but tonight it feels like a king's palace.

I've only ever seen it from the street, its red façade and columns as aloof and imposing as a cathedral. Now I'm standing inside, wearing a borrowed dress, and balancing a flute of champagne like a prop I don't know the cues for. Rachel says I'm fine, and reassures me that I look like I belong there. But Rachel always says that, because Rachel has never once been poor, and she's been raised in circles like this.

The satin of the borrowed gown clings in ways that make me feel every flaw. It's the kind of dress that turns heads, deep green and glossy, but it isn't mine. It doesn't even feel like fabric I should touch without wearing gloves. When I first zipped it up in her bedroom mirror, I thought, this is how women disguise themselves. The bodice is snug enough that I keep reminding myself to breathe through my ribs. My toes, trapped in gold heels, have gone numb.

"Money loves confidence," Rachel whispered as we came in together. "Stand up straight, sip slowly, and pretend this is your life."

But it isn't my life. My life is Amelia's school permission slips, and Sophie's tantrums over the wrong color socks, and pasta dinners eaten standing up because the table is still covered in half-finished art projects, and the sound of the dishwasher rattling like it might give up for good. My life is the rent, due again in two weeks, and the email from my boss telling me there won't be extra hours after all, and the quiet calculation of groceries against what's left in my account.

Here in this room, no one has to count like I do. Their laughter is sharp and easy, and they don't care who hears it. They drift in pairs, in their polished shoes and silk dresses, with their ostentatious jewelry catching the chandelier light. Their voices echo against the domed ceiling, overlapping in a hum that sounds like another language entirely.

I find a painting to hide beside. It's a winter scene, with snow spread across a forest clearing, and a lodge crouched in the shadow of pines. The brushstrokes are precise and studied, like the artist wanted the air to look as cold as it feels outside tonight. A lone figure moves across the snow with a dog at his side. But something about it bothers me. The snow is neat and untouched, like poured sugar on a cake. The birds in the tree branch lift off as if rehearsed, but not one mark mars the whiteness.

I lean closer, tracing the varnish glare with my eyes, and whisper to myself before I can stop.

"Pretty, but fake."

The words hang there, half-swallowed by the air. I squeeze

my glass stem tighter, embarrassed, and take another sip. The champagne is flat on my tongue, bitter in a way I don't quite know if I like. My instinct is to apologize, even though no one heard. At least, I think no one did.

Then there's a stir behind me, and I feel a breath, warm against my neck. There's someone standing closer than strangers usually stand at these things. My body stiffens, but I don't turn. I fix my eyes on the painting as if the figure and his dog might suddenly leave tracks if I stare hard enough. My cheeks flush hot.

And then the presence is gone, as though they've folded back into the crowd. I let out a breath and risk a glance sideways. I catch the retreating glimpse of a black sleeve, the back of a head turning away. My heart taps quickly. I'm ridiculous, I tell myself. Talking to paintings, jumping at shadows.

"Stop glaring at the frame."

Rachel has appeared at my elbow, sparkling in her navy dress, hair sleek and perfect. She smells faintly of jasmine and champagne. "You'll get us banned from every gallery in Boston."

"I wasn't glaring," I protest.

"You were muttering at it." She narrows her eyes playfully. "What was the verdict?"

"It looks staged. Like a winter for people who've never had their socks soak through on the walk to school. Pretty, but...soulless."

Rachel tilts her head, considering. "I like it. But then again, I like staged. Staged usually means catered."

Her grin is sharp enough to make me laugh. It slips out before I can stop it, surprising me with how it feels to seem light, for a second, like I haven't in weeks.

"Anyway," Rachel goes on. "You're doing fine. I've already told three donors you're fascinating."

"Rachel," I warn, but she's already twinkling.

"One thinks you're an art critic writing under a pseudonym. One thinks you left hedge funds because they bored you. One thinks you're my cousin visiting from France who refuses to speak English."

I stare. "Why would you say that?"

"Because no one here listens long enough to know the difference," she says. "And because the real you is infinitely more interesting, but sometimes it helps to borrow a little armor."

The weight in my chest loosens a fraction. Armor, that's all I need. I take another sip of champagne and let the bubbles prick the back of my throat.

"How are the girls?" she asks softly, the joking tone fading.

"Amelia has declared war on long division. Sophie thinks her teacher has vampire teeth." I smile faintly. "They're with Thomas tonight."

Rachel's mouth twists. "Reliable as ever?"

I shrug. "He texted he was running late. Which could mean anything from ten minutes to crossing the border and reinventing himself."

"Don't," she says. "Don't give him that much intrigue."

I nod, but the truth presses behind my ribs. The divorce may be official on paper, but it still feels raw, like a tooth missing in my mouth that my tongue can't leave alone. It's been three months, and the word ex-husband doesn't feel real, but neither does husband anymore. All I know is what's left in the middle. The math of balancing bills and making lunches and the girls' small sorrows.

I look back at the painting again, staring at the figure in the snow who's still moving, and still leaving no tracks. I wonder what kind of world it is where you can walk across snow and it not be marked.

"Stop hiding back here," Rachel says, slipping her hand

briefly over mine on the champagne flute. "This is your night too."

"I don't think this room has a place for women like me," I murmur.

"Correction," she says firmly. "It needs women like you. They just don't know it yet."

She straightens as a couple approaches, her hostess smile blooming.

"Ellen, meet Marion and Paul Isham. They practically built this wing back up with their generosity."

I paste on the polite expression I've learned. We exchange hands and pleasantries, and smiles that mean everything and nothing. Paul gestures toward the painting.

"You were studying this one," he says. "I admire the austerity of it."

"It's beautiful," I say quickly, then add before I can stop myself. "But a little staged. I always look for something imperfect. Something that proves the artist once got cold fingers, or slipped, or laughed while he was painting."

There's a pause. Marion's eyes brighten. Paul only chuckles, raising his glass. "Perfection has its charm," he says. "But I suppose a little flaw never hurts."

The conversation drifts to donations and the quartet playing Mozart. Rachel keeps it buoyant, gliding from subject to subject, looping me in only when necessary. I nod, smile, say the right things. When they drift away again, Rachel leans close.

"You see?" she murmurs. "You don't need my lies. You're interesting enough all on your own."

I shake my head, half laughing, half dazed. "I insulted the painting in front of a major donor."

"You made them remember you," she corrects. "There's a difference."

She moves on, catching someone else's attention with the

effortless poise I'll never have. I linger in front of the winter scene, half hidden again in its shadow. And then I feel that prickling awareness at the back of my neck again. The sensation of eyes on me. Still, I don't turn. I don't want to give them the satisfaction. Instead, I study the brushstrokes harder, whispering the same words to myself under my breath like a prayer.

"Pretty, but fake."

It starts with my own words coming back to me, carried on a voice that sounds like a cello being tuned in a cold room.

"Pretty, but fake," he says behind me, as if tasting the phrase. "That seems to be the requirement for most people here."

I hold my position, not wanting to do the startled-bird jump I've done my whole life when a deeper voice enters a quiet space. I place my fingertips lightly on the gilt of the frame, just enough to steady, not enough to smudge, and give myself the single beat it takes to decide who I am going to be when I face him. Then I pivot.

He's far closer than I expected, which is probably why I felt the warmth of his breath earlier. The gala's low gold light skims over him in planes, lighting on his cheekbone, brow, the clean angle of a jaw freshly shaved into obedience. He is in a black jacket that fits the way most jackets don't fit, the bow tie somehow both careless and perfectly correct. He has dark hair, and eyes the color of old green glass.

There's something in the vowels when he says, "Good evening," too. A faint flattening of the sound, like the sanded edge of a foreign language. Not exactly British, but not Boston, either. A European school somewhere that taught him to eat with three forks and look as if nothing surprises him.

"Good evening," I say back, and try to say it as if I'm comfortable in this dress and in my skin and in a room where the walls expect museum-level composure. He gestures with his chin toward the canvas, a small, private movement.

"You don't like it."

I glance back at the winter scene with its poised birds, the lodge, the man with the dog floating on his own white world, and feel the old reflex to apologize. To retreat from my opinion.

"I didn't say that."

"You said, 'pretty, but fake.'" His mouth moves in a not-smile. Not unfriendly, but more like amusement he's decided to allow. "I have very good ears, even with a quartet sawing at Mozart."

Heat taps at the crown of my head.

"I was…talking to the frame," I say, which is both the truth and ridiculous.

"The frame is a terrible conversationalist," he returns. "Surely, I am better."

He steps half a pace nearer, not enough to invade, just enough to claim equal rights to this small patch of parquet and air. The chandelier light catches the tiniest scratch at the corner of his right eyebrow, marking a pale, healed crescent. An old story there I'll never hear. Or maybe I will.

"Do you want me to lie?" I ask, before my good sense can present its usual slide deck. "Or do you want me to say what I see?"

He looks directly at me, and the room narrows to a little aisle of sight between his pupils and mine.

"Always the second," he says. "It is rare."

"You must not know many five-year-olds," I say, mostly to ease the tightness in my throat. "My Sophie always says exactly what she sees, and then demands a snack as reward."

Something flickers across his face that looks like surprise, then interest, then that same amused allowance.

"It's Ellen, yes?" he says.

It shouldn't be unnerving that he knows my name. After all, Rachel introduces me all the time. Still, the air tilts.

"Yes," I say. "And you are...?"

"Stuart." He lets it sit there for a heartbeat and then adds, as if it matters less, "Stuart Drummond."

The name lands with the soft thud of recognition. I've seen it in brochures and on the bottom of emails that ask for money for libraries or parks. Drummond like the Adirondacks. Drummond like old timber and even older money. I try to keep my face from announcing that a small alarm has gone off in a corner of my brain labeled You Don't Belong Here, Do Not Touch Anything Else.

Rachel is at the far end of the room talking to a donor in a plaid blazer nobody should forgive, but I feel her antennae twitch even from here. Her eyes flick over. She sees me with a man who has that last name. She sees him with me. She lifts one shoulder half an inch in a gesture I've learned means are you okay?

I am, I tell her with a blink. Or I will be.

"You're the donor," I say to Stuart, because that is the obvious assumption.

His mouth does that almost-smile again.

"Sometimes." He tilts his head toward the painting. "Tonight, I am the artist."

The words take a second to cross the space and slot into the correct mental folder. I look from him to the canvas and back. I am not sure what expression I am wearing, but I'm hoping it's something between apology and startle.

"You painted this?" I say, to make sure the law of reality still holds.

"I did."

He doesn't look at the painting when he says it. He looks at me. A normal person would say I'm sorry now. Or at least, oh, I didn't mean to offend. But my brain does that unhelpful thing where it trips into honesty precisely when a polite half-lie would be smoothest.

"It is beautiful," I say, because that is still true. "And I... I guess I just wanted to see where the painter's hand slipped. Maybe that's sentimental."

"Ah. I see."

He steps closer to the frame, studying it as if he's never seen it before. The scent of him is expensive, hinting of clean shirt, and cedar maybe, but not cologne so much as the memory of wood.

"You are looking for a pulse."

"Yes," I say, relieved that he's handed me a word. "Yes. A pulse."

He nods once, slow. "Most people look for perfection. They come to the canvas wanting proof that winter can be captured, the way you capture a fly in amber." His voice smooths that last word into a longer, rolling end, the r slender and unhurried. "It pleases them to see it without the parts that make it loud."

"Loud?" I echo, curious despite myself.

"Snow is loud," he says, and for a moment he is not in this room at all. He is somewhere else with the collar turned up on his coat, a forest taking the sound from his breath and giving it back in a different key. "It shouts when it falls and it roars when it melts and it makes the smallest sounds violent. Your own feet are like a drum. In a museum, people prefer the silence."

He slides his hands into his pockets, the tailor somewhere in heaven sighing with pleasure at that small movement.

"I didn't give them footprints because I like that lie."

"Lie?" I repeat.

He looks at me then, all the way, as if we're the only two witnesses to a private joke.

"Where I grew up, we didn't leave tracks."

It should be a harmless sentence, except it isn't. Something in my old animal place stiffens. The words feel polished from being held in the mouth too often, and something about the way he says it makes his past sound like a threat. But his gaze is steady and open, not cruel. I watch the line of his throat move when he swallows.

"Maybe I'm wrong," I say, because I have a reflex to tug the conversational plane back to level. "I don't know. Maybe I want every painting to have a rip in the seam."

"Most do." The almost-smile again, closer to real now. "You simply need to know where to pull."

He shifts, just enough that his shoulder is almost touching mine. I realize that we have drifted to the edge of the alcove without my noticing, and the reading room opens behind us like a stage we have stepped off. The bust of some dead white poet watches from a pedestal as if approving this smaller theater.

"Come," he says quietly, and it's not a command so much as an invitation spoken in a tone that makes you want to accept. He moves toward the half-screened side of the alcove, where a smaller painting hangs much lower on the wall than the rest, as if meant for a different audience. I follow, because I am not rude, and because my curiosity is a dog that comes the moment it hears its name.

This one is a study. Its brushwork is looser, and the color less mannered. A scrap of winter with a length of fence half-buried, a hunched fox in the mid-distance turning its face back, the sky the violet color of and early bruise. In the foreground, there's the rough suggestion of a footprint, then another, then a third, fading under a fine sift of new snow. It is imperfect and alive. I make a small sound I don't intend. He doesn't react to the sound itself, but to what made it.

"You see?" he says, and his voice is softer.

"I do," I say, matching the softness, unwilling to spook

whatever this feeling is. It's a moment of recognition that isn't about men or money or rooms, but just about seeing something that matches the shape in your mind. "You kept this one honest."

"Honest doesn't sell as well," he says, and there's humor in it but no complaint. "People want to buy the idea that the world obeys them."

"I keep trying to sell that to my five-year-old," I say. "She isn't buying."

"You mentioned a Sophie." He holds my gaze the way a good interviewer holds a pause. "You have more than one child?"

"Two girls." I hear the familiar pride in my voice before I can tamp it down. It does something to his face—like lighting a match behind frosted glass. "Ten and five. Amelia and Sophie."

"Amelia," he repeats, and the vowels turn newly elegant in his mouth. "A serious name."

"She would agree with you." I wonder why I am giving this away. Because of the alcove, because of the painting that allowed for footprints, because he is looking at me like my answer matters more than the stages of his own career. "They're with their father tonight."

"The divorce was recent," he says, not as a question.

"Yes." I realize, too late, that I've been rubbing at the edge of my empty champagne flute with my thumb the whole time and the motion has a fretful look to it. I lower my hand. "We are... adjusting. It's a lot of math."

"Math," he says, amused. "Not grief."

"That too," I say. The word lands heavy, but he doesn't flinch. "Math is easier to talk about at a gala."

His mouth curves, but I am suddenly aware that his eyes have not left my face for more than a second at a time since he said hello. It isn't predatory, which would be simple to file. It's attentive in a way that feels both flattering and slightly dangerous. As if, by focusing so hard, he could bend the evening into the shape he prefers.

"What do you do, Ellen?" he asks. The question is threaded with the same focus. "Besides reorganize the gravitational field for two small planets."

"I write," I say, and then hear the old instinct in my own voice to undercut it with a little joke, a little self-effacement on the side, so no one thinks you are thinking too much of yourself. I swallow it back. "I write and I help other people write. I pick through their words and put them where they belong. I build stories that are hiding inside other stories."

He turns his head slightly, as if to hear better. "Ah. I like this. Story as architecture."

"And demolition," I say, surprised to hear myself add it. "Sometimes you have to knock down the walls to find the rot."

He laughs then, a short, genuine sound that sits warm for a moment in the cold alcove. "You would be dangerous in a studio," he says. "You would point at the wall and say, 'Here. Hit this.'"

"I would say, 'Here. Push this.'" I realize that my hands have come up, explaining. I fold them, the green satin of the borrowed bodice whispering when I move. "And I would probably be wrong sometimes."

"Wrong is only more interesting," he says. "Wrong is a door." He considers me in the same way he considered the smaller canvas, with a professional curiosity that contains a filament of something else. "You said you wanted a pulse. Will you help me find it?"

I blink. "In this painting?"

"In others," he says simply. "In what comes next." He leans one shoulder against the shadowed wall, the pose practiced but not performative. "I am supposed to be assembling a body of work for a show. Some new pieces, and plenty of old ones that need to be... unstiffened. An irritating word I promised I wouldn't say in public, but there it is."

It lands like both an offer and a test. A little electricity snakes up under my ribs, like hope braided with caution. I am at a gala in a dress that is not mine, and a man with a family name that bends rooms is asking me, in a voice that makes verbs sound warmer than they are, to come closer to his work.

"Is this a job offer?" I ask lightly, because lightness makes it safer to hear the answer.

"It is an invitation," he says. "To speak plainly, as you did just now, in a space where people seldom do. To stand with me in front of canvases and tell me where to pull at the seam." He tilts his head. "I would pay you for your time, of course. I dislike the American habit of asking women to give away their intelligence for exposure."

The part of me that has done exactly that, who has written a thousand unpaid words for the promise of later, wants to shake his hand on the spot. The part of me that still smells the sharp iron in the air of my old life reminds me to slow down. Ask a better question.

"Why me?" I ask.

His gaze flicks, briefly, to my mouth and back, and I feel the blush rise like a stupid schoolgirl's. "Because you looked at something expensive and asked it to be honest," he says. "Because you did not look at me when you said it."

"That was an accident," I say, and he shrugs, unconvinced.

Across the reading room, somewhere between the quartet and the marble stairs, Rachel's laugh arcs like a tossed coin. When I find her again, she is not laughing. She is watching us from the corner of her eye as she nods at something a donor is saying. Her fingers touch the chain at her throat in a gesture I have learned means she is filing away a thought she may not like.

"Can I think about it?" I ask him. "The invitation."

"Of course." He produces a small, unadorned card from a jacket pocket. It bears no title, and no logo, just a name and a number written in a thin, impatient hand. He doesn't offer it palm-out the way people do. He holds it out between two fingers like an object with weight. When I take it, our fingers brush. The touch is nothing and it is not nothing at the same time.

"Call me tomorrow," he says, very low, without giving me instructions the way men sometimes do. No I'll expect your call at nine, no I have a slot at noon. Just a simple imperative wrapped in courtesy. "Or don't. If you do not, I will assume your life is full and that will please me in its way."

He straightens, as if the conversation has run its perfect course. For a second, I think he will walk back into the crowd and dissolve. Instead, he looks past my shoulder, at the staged winter, and says, almost to himself, "Perfection is a kind of cruelty, don't you think?"

I want to ask, To whom? To the viewer? To the artist? To the people in the painted house? But he is already moving away, and the crowd swallows and releases him like tide water around a rock. I am left in the alcove with the honest fox and the lie of the lodge and a card with his name dark against my sweat-damp palm.

"Who was that?" Rachel has ghosted to my side in the way only women who have learned to cross a room invisibly can. Her smile is public-facing but her eyes are not. She does not look at the card, but her gaze knows it is there.

"Stuart Drummond," I say, and her breath catches imperceptibly on the second syllable.

"The painter," she says, which is confirmation, and something she does with the corners of her mouth is not quite approval. "And the patron. And, perhaps most importantly, the Drummond."

"Apparently all three," I say.

"What did he want?"

"To hire me," I say, and it sounds like a game when I say it that way, like I'm a character who has wandered onto a nicer set. Rachel's lashes lower and lift.

"Oh, did he now?"

A waiter breezes by and she plucks a fresh glass from the tray, then thinks better of it and trades it to me.

"Hydrate," she says as cover, and then adds, even softer, so it can't be heard by anyone but me and the bust of the dead poet.

"He had a way of looking like you were the only thing in the room that makes sound."

"He listened," I say, aware of the defensive note and wishing it weren't there. "He asked about Amelia and Sophie."

"Dangerous," she murmurs.

"What?"

"Men who notice you have children," she says in that same almost-nothing voice. "They know it's the fastest map to a woman's heart."

I look at her, waiting for the rest, waiting for her to add that he's messy, he's mean, he's wonderful, he's married. But she doesn't give it. Rachel is a generous storyteller but also a good one. She knows when to let the chapter break on the page turn.

"If he calls me 'pretty, but fake' I'll throw this champagne on him," I say, and she smiles with her teeth but not her eyes.

"You will not throw anything," she says. "You will consider the offer. You will ask for a rate that makes him blink. You will remember that his attention is a force field and you should step out of it occasionally to check your footing."

Beyond us, the quartet swells into something lush. The chandeliers do their old tired glitter. The winter on the wall keeps pretending to be quiet, and the honest fox keeps looking back from its own small world as if to ask, Are you sure?

"I'm sure of nothing," I say to Rachel, and to the painting, and to the card in my hand. "But I'm here."

She loops her arm through mine the way she had in the coatroom.

"That," she says. "Is the hardest part."

We step back into the reading room's current. People move around us with that gala-specific grace, their conversations made glossy by money, warmth, and champagne. I can feel the press of Stuart's focus still, like a hand that hovered and has only just withdrawn. I'm careful not to look for him, not to prove Rachel right. The card thins in my sweaty palm, as if it wants to escape or melt.

"Will you go to his studio?" Rachel asks lightly, as if this is a question about a sale rack or a new bakery.

"Maybe," I say, which is the safest answer and the truest. I think of the smaller painting with the fading prints. I think of the word he used, cruelty, and how easily it slid into the space between us and sat down.

I close my hand more tightly around the card before it can slip. I tell myself, again, the thing that has gotten me through every morning for months. You showed up. And, because I am honest with myself in a way I haven't been in a long time, I admit the other thing too. There is a part of me that loved being the only sound in the room for him.

2

The flowers are way too big for my hallway. They're wedged on the second-floor landing outside my door. A huge bouquet of roses and lilies and pale frilled things I can't name, muscled together in a glass cylinder. A white card leans from the bouquet's throat like a secret. Mrs. Pell from 2B has already cracked her door to stare.

"For you?" she calls, delighted the way people get when someone else's fortune arrives by mistake.

"I guess," I say, though I don't know anyone who sends flowers this size unless someone died. And no one has died. My keys jingle against the lock. The vase is heavier than it looks. I shoulder the door open and carry it in like a newborn.

Our apartment looks exactly as it did when I left it. There are crayons in a jelly jar, paper crowns strung along the curtain rod, the discolored patch of wax on the kitchen table where Sophie tried to "iron" with a hot spoon. The radiator ticks gently like an animal sleeping. I set the bouquet on the counter by the sink and the room shrinks a little around it, as if the arrangement brought in a demand for its own square footage.

The girls' artwork on the fridge watches me accept the kind

of gift that belongs in a hotel lobby. I pull the card free. No logo and no imprinted boutique font. Just my name in an impatient hand and below it, a line that says:

Thank you for telling the snow the truth. Dinner? — S.

It is exactly like him to make six words feel like a guiding hand on your arm. I breathe in the flowers because that's what people do, but they smell expensive more than anything else. The girls are with Thomas until Sunday morning, which means I'm alone with the quiet apartment and a note from a man who rearranged the air around me last night simply by paying attention.

The card trembles a little between my fingers. How did he get my address? A quick dart of alarm and then the easy answer. Rachel. She promised to pass along my "details" to new clients. She would absolutely trade my address for the possibility of my next invoice. I tell myself that's what happened. I tell myself this kind of floral gesture is old-fashioned, not invasive.

I set the note on the counter, and text Rachel anyway. He sent flowers, I type. They look like they ate a smaller bouquet on the way over. Two dots pulse, then the little bubble appears. Oh? she writes. And?

And a note asking me out to dinner.

There's a pause. Are you going? I don't answer her. Instead, I call him. He picks up on the third ring.

"Ellen," he says, my name dark in his voice like a chocolate left in the sun. "Good. You got them."

"They're pretty hard to miss." I look around my kitchen that tries so hard to be a kitchen. The flowers look like they were flown business-class. "They're...beautiful. Thank you."

"A blunt instrument," he says, amused. "But useful. Dinner tomorrow? Or do your small planets exert their gravity?"

"Tomorrow I'm free." The words come out easier than they should. "Seven?"

"Seven-thirty," he says, decisive. "I will send you the address. If you want me to collect you, I can."

"No." It comes out a little fast. "I'll meet you there."

"Good." I hear the smile even if he doesn't let it fully form. "Wear the green again."

The call ends. I stand in my kitchen with the phone in my palm and the bouquet on the counter and a part of me that is usually careful making an indulgent sound.

The restaurant he texts is tucked into a brownstone in Back Bay. It's one of those places that never has to explain itself because the plates are heavy and the light is low and the waiters glide in shoes that don't squeak. The next night, my heels bite my toes again and the zipper at my side purrs a little warning. I wear the green because he asked, and I tell myself I chose it.

He's already there when I walk in, talking to the maître d' with the easy patience of someone who doesn't ever have their patience tested. He turns toward me and the room edits itself so that for three seconds everything else is a blur. I'm not naïve enough to believe in chemistry like a fairy tale, but I am old enough to recognize that some people have learned how to cast. His attention lands and leaves a warmth.

"You came," he says, as if there was a real possibility I wouldn't.

"I did."

"Good." He takes in the dress, the hair I've redone twice in the bathroom mirror. "And you wore the green," he says, satisfied, and then, it's so small as a gesture, but his fingers touch my shoulder near the strap.

"Here," he murmurs, almost to himself. "Lengthen a little."

He runs one knuckle up between my shoulder blades, not intimate, but the way a teacher might remind you to lift your chin at a piano recital. I comply without thinking, spine rising, throat opening. People don't understand how many of us have been trained from birth to obey small corrections. He smiles. Not at my body, but at the obedience of it.

"You're luminous when you remember you are tall," he says.

I hear the sentence and store it, because this is how it begins. With a compliment wearing the coat of a command.

He asks if he can order for both of us, and I say yes, grateful to be relieved of another decision. Dishes arrive that I would never choose because they are all the things that frighten my grocery budget. He watches my face when I taste them, curious in the way men who have never had to do arithmetic are curious about the physics of a different life. He tells me very little about himself, he is much better at asking about me. He makes me talk about my daughters as if Amelia and Sophie were artworks he wants to understand. What color their tempers are, which brushstrokes soothe them, where the accidental paint is, the part worth preserving exactly as it is.

"Amelia is... precise," I say. "She takes a ruler to the world and writes notes in the margins. Sophie, on the other hand, is all margins and no rules."

He laughs, delighted like a person who is not, actually, used to children. "Margins are where the good drawings are to be found," he says, and I want to kiss him for saying it, which is stupid. Instead, I talk about piano lessons I can't afford and the science kit that stained our carpet green. I hear myself editing out the parts that sound like complaint and keeping the parts that make us glow.

When the bill comes, I reach for my purse out of muscle memory and he catches my wrist midair with a look that says, don't insult us both. As we stand, he checks my back again with the lightest touch, reminding me to lengthen my spine, and then we're moving out into January air sharp enough to sand the mouth. He offers a car home. I say no out of habit, he makes a small gentle face, then walks me to the corner anyway, hands in pockets, a man who knows his silhouette against a streetlight. He doesn't kiss me goodnight. He kisses the space next to my face, the hint of my jaw. It is both old-fashioned and proprietary. I go home warm and a little warning-bell cold.

What follows is not a whirlwind, because whirlwinds are messy. This is far more tailored. Tickets appear in my mailbox in a gray envelope with my name written as if the letters were tired of being separate from one another. A note: Theatre. Bring R. Or don't. The seats are excellent and Rachel leans in while the lights are still up and whispers, "Well, someone wants something."

"What if he just wants me to see a play?" I say.

"No one has ever *just* wanted anything."

We watch without talking through most of Act I, except for the part where the set slides and the actors stop pretending to project winter and I feel it settle over me, that stage cold that isn't cold at all. At intermission we walk to the lobby where the carpet is always uglier than the audience, and Stuart is already there, somehow between conversations. He doesn't push. He doesn't do the arm-around-claim in public. He touches one finger to the silk scarf I borrowed from Rachel, brow furrowing slightly, affectionate, critical. "This shade fights you," he says softly, a lover's diagnosis. "Next time, bone, not cream."

I feel my face flicker through surprise, then obedience, then annoyance at the obedience. "It's Rachel's," I say.

"Then she can have it back," he replies, amused. "And I'll buy you the right one."

He hands me a tiny envelope with two drink tickets and makes it seem like a gift instead of the oldest trick in a lobby. Rachel slips away under the pretense of a bathroom line that is miraculously short. When she returns, she stands the way she stands when something has bothered her and she's refused to let it ruin her lipstick.

"Is he always like that?" she asks, as we watch him drift away to greet someone he doesn't need to impress.

"Like what?"

"Like he knows how you should hold your own neck." She mimics his earlier gesture on my spine with theatrical exaggeration. "It's performative chivalry at best."

"He's an artist," I say, and even to my own ears it sounds like a soft defense. "He looks at things."

"That doesn't mean he gets to rearrange them in public," she says, and then softens. "Please don't move too fast. Men like that come on like weather."

The second week he brings pastries to my door at eight a.m. on a Saturday, and the knock is so gentle I almost don't hear it. I'm in pajama pants and a T-shirt that says Ask Me About My Cat even though I don't own a cat. My hair has made decisions I wasn't consulted on. I open the door and he's there in a fine coat, holding a white box with a ribbon, the like of which I've only seen in shop windows.

"Good morning," he says, delighted by the sight of me undone. He looks at me, not with pity or scorn, but with a kind of surprise that feels like the first time you see a favorite painting without glass. I can tell that he didn't expect to like this version and does. "I was near."

"In Boston?" I ask, skeptical.

"In your zip code," he corrects, grinning.

I should feel intruded upon. I should remind him of boundaries. Instead, I invite him in, and greedily, I open the box on the kitchen table like a magician's assistant. The girls dive at the glossy pastries with reverence I've never seen them apply to anything edible. Amelia, who can be rigidly polite, says "thank you" without being prompted. Sophie's shyness does something I haven't seen before. She looks at him as if he was an animal she wants to draw and then hides behind the refrigerator door.

He crouches to their level with unpracticed knees.

"My name's Stuart," he says to the tile because neither girl can manage eye contact. "You must be the rule-maker," he tells Amelia gently, and she, surprised into a smile she doesn't give strangers, nods once.

"And you?" He doesn't try to coax Sophie out. He slides a napkin across the table, pulls a pencil from his coat pocket as if that is a normal thing a man carries, and draws a fox in nine quick strokes. He does not sign it, which is the most impressive thing he does all morning. Sophie peeks. She peeks again.

"It's looking back," she whispers.

"They often do," he says. He pushes the napkin a fraction closer. "You can keep it. If you want."

She keeps it. She tapes it to the fridge next to a purple planet and declares no one can move it because the fox must be near cold things. Amelia thanks him again and then goes back to categorizing pastries by crumble factor as if she intends to publish a thesis.

He does not stay long. He kisses the air near my ear again, smiles at the girls in a way that makes them not flinch, and calls over his shoulder as he goes, "Stand tall, Ellen," as if posture is prayer and he is the priest.

After he leaves, the apartment warms in a way that is not just radiators and sugar. Amelia watches me watching the door and narrows her eyes the way she does when we are doing math and she suspects the problem has a trick.

"I like him," she says in a voice that already knows how to be cautious. "But I don't know him yet."

"That's fair," I say, because I don't either.

Sophie drifts back into view, fox-napkin now clutched in her small hand.

"He smells like snow," she announces, not quite approving,

but not quite disapproving either. She's just making a note, the way children do, to revisit the thought later.

By the third week there are hotel lobbies. He likes them the way some men like garages, because they're spaces that promise cleanliness and function and a certain show of power. We meet once at a place in Back Bay where the floors are so polished the lamps glow in them. He's reading a notebook whose pages are bloated with paint smears and taped scraps.

"I had an hour," he says by way of greeting. "And I didn't want to waste it." He looks at me like the hour has improved.

A server appears. He orders for us without asking what I want and somehow gets it right, choosing a gin I like because it tastes like someone happened to pick rosemary outside your door. When I reach for the little dish of almonds, he moves it closer, efficient as a caretaker, and then fixes the clasp of my necklace where it has rotated to hide behind my collarbone.

"There," he says, which is both helpful and a proprietary word pretending to be helpful.

"It didn't need fixing," I say lightly.

"Everything needs to be seen in the right light," he replies. He isn't wrong. It is the reason the hotel built this lobby.

There are theatre tickets again. "For when you remember to be the woman who likes theatre," his note says. And a surprise string quartet in a bar so narrow we have to turn sideways to let the cellist through. He introduces me to people without giving me context and, somehow, they all know my name.

"This is Ellen," he says with that attentive heat, and I become Ellen the way he says her. I am not immune to being renamed.

Rachel is not immune, either, but for different reasons.

"He's... a lot," she says, finally, over coffee in a café with chairs that wobble and a bathroom key attached to a colander. "And yes, he is gracious, and yes, he is persuasive, and yes, I am a cynic who has dated too many men who thought the world was their studio." She takes my hand, very nearly pleading. "Please don't let his focus convince you it is love. Focus like that is a spotlight, and you can't always see the edges it blots out."

"Why do you always assume the worst?" I ask, but I make it sound half-joking.

"Because it keeps me alive," she says, and then realizes she has been more dramatic than she meant. "Because I want you well. Because anyone who notices the angle of your eyelashes in public and corrects your necklace like he's your dresser, is auditioning for a part too soon."

"He's just European," I say, which might be the laziest defense I've ever made. "Maybe it's just... good manners."

"Or control wrapped in manners," she counters. "I didn't say he's awful. I said slow down. Make him earn the next scene."

I nod because it's easy and because she loves me. Then I ignore her because it's easier and because I want this in a way I haven't wanted anything in a very long time. The wanted-ness feels like oxygen after standing up too fast. It occurs to me that oxygen can also be anesthetic.

On a Thursday that feels like a Friday because I haven't slept enough, he shows up outside my building without warning, carrying two cups of hot chocolate in a paper tray. I'm annoyed for a second. I have just got back from dropping the children at school, and I have dishes to do, laundry to sort, words to write. And then I see him under the vestibule light with steam curling from the cups and the annoyance becomes a small, traitorous delight.

"Walk?" he asks, offering me the choice like it's not the only option.

I say yes. He hands me a cup and it is the exact temperature my hands want. We walk three blocks nowhere special while he tells me about a canvas that won't behave and I tell him about Sophie's meltdown at school because someone took the green crayon she'd already named. When we stop at the corner to say goodbye, he touches my shoulder again. Not there this time, but a little higher, his thumb skimming the fine place where neck becomes jaw.

"Up," he says.

"Up?" I echo.

"Your chin. The world does not deserve the inside of your throat. Save that for people who know what it's for."

For a half second, I consider telling him that my throat belongs to me, that I can tilt it any way I want. Instead, I lift my chin like a good student, and he smiles like a good teacher, and the red flag flutters so prettily I tell myself it's a ribbon.

I go upstairs, and lift the fox drawing from where it's fluttered to the floor, straightening the corners, and pinning in back on the fridge with a bold magnet. I check Amelia's workbook and circle a correct answer as if she needed my permission to be right. My phone buzzes. It's Rachel.

Still alive? she texts.

Better than that, I write back before I can talk myself into humility. I'm being entertained.

~

Boston Common is a different kind of stage once the daylight slides off its shoulders. The tourists thin out, the benches empty, and the lamps flicker on with a kind of weary sigh. It smells like damp grass and old stone, the faint, fruity tang of the river riding the air.

We walk slowly, as if the evening has given us permission to meander. Stuart matches his pace to mine, his coat brushing my sleeve every few steps. There are still enough people around to make the walk feel public and safe, but not enough to keep me from noticing how closely his attention fixes on me, as if no one else exists.

"It's strange," he says, gazing up through the branches of an oak that creaks with the weight of spring's refusal to arrive. "All these years I've painted Boston from a distance. The skyline, the river, the way the Common swells with people in summer. But I've rarely just walked through it. Feet on the ground. It's too simple, maybe."

"Simple isn't bad," I say. "I'd take simple over... well, pretty much everything else."

He glances at me, curious. His eyes catch the lamplight like polished stone. "Everything else?"

The words hang there, waiting. I sip the air and try to remember when I last told anyone the truth without sanding down the rough edges.

"My marriage," I admit finally. "It was never simple. Not in the good ways. It was always a negotiation about money, or time, or who's doing what. Who's failing whom." I give a little laugh, thin as tissue. "I used to think stability meant pretending everything was fine. Keeping the girls quiet, the house tidy, the dinner on the table like a peace offering. I was wrong."

He doesn't interrupt. He doesn't look away, either. His silence isn't careless, it's deliberate, coaxing more out of me. I keep going.

"I left with two suitcases, a box of toys, and the hope that I could keep them safe. That was the trade I made. Safe but broke. Stable but exhausted."

We pause near the bridge where the swan boats hibernate under canvas. A gust stirs the water into shivers and I hug my coat tighter. He doesn't offer to shield me from the cold, he just studies me like a painting he can't quite decide if he loves.

"Safe," he repeats softly. "That's what you give them. That is your art, Ellen."

I almost laugh at the word art in relation to me, who can barely stretch rent some months. But he says it with such gravity that it feels momentarily true.

"You sound lonely," he adds. "Even when you're describing love."

"That's because I am." The admission slips out before I can stop it. It's the kind of comment I usually swallow down, or cover with a joke. But his gaze makes swallowing impossible. "There's no time for... anyone else. Just work and the girls and..." I trail off.

"And now me." His smile is small, almost reverent. "If you'll allow it."

We keep walking. The gravel crunches under our shoes, the sound almost intimate in the quiet. The garden lamps halo the air in soft gold, and I feel suspended in a place that could vanish if I move too suddenly.

"Were you lonely before?" I ask. "Before tonight?"

He breathes out as though the question has been waiting for him. "Always. Since I was a boy. People see the money, the name, the paintings They see what they want to consume. But they don't see me. Not as I am." His voice dips lower. "Except you."

I want to say, you don't even know me. But some reckless part of me thrills at the idea that maybe he does.

"I've had lovers," he continues, almost confessional. "They wanted the artist, the Drummond name, the myth. None of them wanted to hear about the snow that never leaves tracks, or the silence that howls in a house too big for one person. None of them wanted to hear about the boy who grew up watching his mother run through the trees, knowing she would never escape."

I blink, startled. He hasn't spoken of family before. There's an edge in his tone, darker than the lamps can touch. I picture the forest in his painting, the house, the figure in the snow with no footsteps. My skin prickles.

"I don't want to bore you," he says, softer again, as if he's caught himself stepping close to something raw.

"You're not boring me," I assure him, even though my stomach has tightened. "You're... different from anyone I've met."

His hand brushes mine. Not a grab, not even a clasp. Just enough to remind me his body is there, charged, ready. The shock of it sends warmth up my arm.

"You see me," he whispers. "That means everything."

I should be careful. I should hear the hunger in his voice not as romance but as warning. But it has been so long since anyone looked at me with attention that feels like a tether, that I can easily mistake it for devotion.

We turn toward the river, where the Charles glimmers under the last fragments of daylight. A couple jogs past us, their breath puffing white, and then we are alone again. Stuart stops near the railing, both hands resting on the iron as though holding himself back.

"You deserve more than exhaustion," he says, voice low. "More than just surviving. I could..." He shakes his head, almost embarrassed. "I could give you something different."

The words should make me wary. They sound like a promise too big for any man to keep. But part of me, the part worn down by endless grocery lists and rent checks, leans into them like warmth.

"What if I don't want different?" I test.

"Then tell me now," he says quickly. His eyes are sharp, searching my face for the truth. "Tell me to stop and I will. I'll vanish. But if you don't..." His hand finds mine properly this time, fingers sliding between my own. His skin is cool. "Then I'll stay."

I don't tell him to stop.

We walk further, hand in hand, the Common behind us and the river opening wide. He asks about the girls again, about Amelia's stubborn streak, Sophie's imagination. I find myself describing them the way I used to write character sketches in college, as if he needs to know every detail before he can paint them in his mind. He listens like the world depends on my words, his eyes intent, hungry.

By the time we reach the corner where the streetlights buzz and traffic claims the night, I've said more to him than I've said to anyone in years. He doesn't kiss me. He just touches my chin, gently tilting it up, the same way he had in the theatre.

"Don't look down when you walk," he says softly. "You belong upright."

It feels like affection and it feels like care. I don't yet recognize it for what it also is. It's possession.

3

The first hint of the weekend is the suitcase. On a Friday morning, I find it leaning against my apartment door like a secret I wasn't meant to uncover yet. It's new, navy leather with brass corners that shine like polished coins, a card tucked into the handle in the same impatient hand as before says: Pack warm. I'll explain later.

I should text him, ask questions, and draw boundaries. I should remind him that I have the girls to look after, and that my time isn't his to claim. But Sophie and Amelia are already with Thomas for the weekend, and his turn was written on the calendar in red for all to see, and the thought of going somewhere, anywhere, that isn't the grocery store or the school run tugs at me like a tide.

When Stuart arrives, he doesn't even ask if I'm ready. He simply takes the suitcase from my hand as though it belongs to him, places it in the back of his immaculate car, and opens the passenger door with a look that tells me hesitation would be an insult.

The drive north is long enough that Boston loosens its grip. Concrete fades to fields, and the traffic hum becomes silence broken only by the whisper of tires against snow-dusted roads. Stuart talks easily, his voice low and steady, as if he's used to filling silences without noticing. He tells me about the mountains he climbed in Switzerland, and about the way frost looks under a painter's lamp, or about the stories colors tell when you mix them wrong. I listen, lulled, the white blur of passing countryside like static in the background.

By the time we reach Vermont, dusk has dropped its blue veil over everything. The inn rises from the snow like something out of a postcard. Its gables are dusted white, and lanterns glow warm in frosted windows, smoke curling from chimneys. Inside, the air is warm enough to sting my cheeks. The lobby smells of woodsmoke, pine, and maple. It makes me want to lick the air.

"Suite for two," Stuart tells the woman at the desk, handing her a key card already waiting in an envelope. Of course, he booked in advance. Of course, everything is seamless.

The suite is larger than my entire apartment. A fire crackles in a stone hearth, armchairs waiting like open arms. The windows stretch tall and bare to the mountains outside, where snow drapes the slopes in folds of silver under moonlight. A basket of fruit waits on the table beside a bottle of wine already breathing into the room.

I laugh, helpless, dizzy. "This is... Stuart, this is too much."

"Too much is only another word for what you deserve," he says, and for a moment I let myself believe it.

There are gifts, too. A sweater softer than anything I own, folded on the bed with tissue paper still clinging to it. A pair of leather gloves in a box so fine I hesitate to touch it. He brushes aside my protests with a kiss to my hair, and a murmur of "indulge me." When I slip the sweater over my head, he stands back as though appraising a painting.

"Yes," he says softly. "Now you look like you belong out here in the snow."

Dinner is in the inn's restaurant, where the beams are dark and heavy and the candles throw gold across the tables. The menu is the kind where prices don't appear, and I don't feel guilty letting him decide what to choose from it. He orders venison for himself, trout for me, as if he knows without asking what I'll prefer. Wine pools in my glass like liquid garnet. I can feel myself loosening under the weight of all the gifts, the good food, the firelight, and the quiet authority of a man who seems to have thought of everything. For the first time since the divorce, I feel like someone wants me not out of obligation but out of choice. Not because I'm the girls' mother, not because I'm reliable, but because I am me.

Later, we sit by the fire in the suite. Snowflakes tick against the glass, faint as moth wings. Stuart stretches his legs, the firelight cutting sharp planes across his face. He looks older in the shadows, but steadier too, like someone carved from the same wood as the beams.

"My mother would have loved this place," he says suddenly, staring into the flames.

I glance at him, surprised by the shift. "She liked Vermont?"

"She liked anywhere the trees outnumbered the people," he says, a faint smile ghosting his mouth. "Isobel was... singular. She believed houses held souls. She used to say a family lodge isn't just timber and stone, it's inheritance. Memory made solid."

There's a hush in his tone, reverence so thick it nearly vibrates. I lean closer, resting my hand on the arm of the chair between us.

"It sounds like you were close."

"Closer than I've been to anyone." His eyes flick to me, then back to the fire. "She taught me to see. Not just with my eyes, but here." He touches his chest with two fingers. "She believed beauty was a responsibility. That if you could capture it, preserve it, you were bound to do so."

I let the words settle. To me it sounds like devotion, the kind of fierce love you carry for someone who shaped you. I don't hear the sharper edge beneath, or the weight of something more consuming.

"She must have been proud of you," I say gently.

"Proud, yes. Demanding." He takes a sip of wine, eyes distant. "She believed no woman would ever understand me the way she did. That perhaps I shouldn't expect it."

I laugh softly, trying to lighten the heaviness of his words.

"That's what mothers are for. To believe they know their children better than anyone else."

But he doesn't laugh. He only watches the fire, and murmurs, "Sometimes I think she was right."

The words should chill me but they don't. I hear only the grief of a son mourning a woman who was his compass. My heart aches for him. I reach across and lay my hand over his.

"You're not alone anymore."

His fingers tighten around mine. His gaze turns to me, and in the glow of the hearth his eyes look almost fevered.

"Don't ever leave," he says, voice low.

I smile, thinking it's the wine, the firelight, the romance of the snow pressing us close.

"I'm not going anywhere," I whisper back.

He kisses me then, fierce and claiming, as if we're sealing a pact I didn't know I'd made.

Later, as I drift toward sleep in the vast bed, the fire still snapping in the grate, I feel warm and wanted in a way I haven't in years. The snow lies heavy on the mountains, and for just a moment, I believe maybe I've found something safe. I don't yet see that what I've mistaken for safety is really a net.

The inn's dining room glows like the inside of a lantern. Shadows curl in the corners while the fire snaps and hisses in its stone throat. Every table has a single candle, tall and white, dripping wax down polished brass. The flame at ours leans slightly, as if straining to overhear us.

Stuart has insisted we dine alone. Not alone as in away from others, since there are other couples murmuring at tables nearby, silverware chiming. But alone as in the staff knows not to intrude. He arranged it with that quiet authority he carries, that never asks twice.

He ordered for us again. I tried to protest, but he only brushed my hand and murmured, "Trust me." And I did. Because when he says it, trust me, it doesn't sound like a request. It sounds inevitable.

The plates arrive filled with roasted duck glistening under a lacquer of orange, vegetables folded into neat bundles, potatoes fanned like pages of a book. I can't remember the last time food looked too beautiful to eat. Maybe never.

I laugh when I take the first bite. "I feel like I should apologize to the chef for ruining the art."

"The chef exists for you," Stuart says simply. "Not the other way around."

He watches me eat more than he eats himself. I should find it unnerving, but instead it feels adoring. The way his gaze lingers, drinking me in, as though he's memorizing not just my face but the way I hold a fork, the way my mouth curves when I taste something I like.

When the plates are cleared and the wine refilled, he leans back in his chair. His eyes are darker in the candlelight, the green receding into shadow. He looks as if he's gathering courage, though it's hard to imagine a man like Stuart lacking it.

"Ellen," he says softly. "There is something I need to ask you."

My heart stumbles. I set down my glass carefully, afraid my hand might betray me with a tremor.

"You must know," he continues. "That before you, there was nothing. Days full of silence, canvases half-finished, the echo of a house that no longer felt alive. I had convinced myself I was meant to endure that solitude forever. Until you."

I open my mouth, but he raises his hand, not to hush me rudely but to hold the moment in suspension.

"You. Your beauty, your strength, your refusal to flatter lies. You are the one who walked into my silence and gave it sound. The one who reminded me that companionship is not a weakness but a salvation." His voice dips lower. "You rescued me, Ellen. Do you know that?"

The room tilts slightly, the candle's flame bowing and rising. My throat is tight. He reaches inside his jacket and pulls out something small, hidden in his palm. He sets it on the table, turning his hand over slowly. A ring glitters against the wood. It's not modest. Not even practical. The stone is large enough to catch the candlelight and scatter it across the tablecloth in fractured stars.

My breath snags. "Stuart."

"Marry me," he says.

Not a question. Not even a plea. A declaration, as if he is giving me the answer before I've spoken the problem aloud. The restaurant hums around us, but in my ears, there is only the rush of my pulse. Weeks. It's only been a matter of weeks. I think of Amelia's cautious smile, Sophie's shy fox drawing taped to the fridge. I think of school lunches, permission slips, the math of rent versus groceries. I think of Rachel's voice. Too fast, Ellen. Too fast.

I open my mouth, and it is Rachel's words that try to climb out first. You don't know him. You don't know what he wants. But Stuart's gaze pins me, steady and unwavering. His eyes are lit with something fierce. It's need, devotion, and desperation all in one, and it makes me feel chosen in a way I have never been.

"Fate brought us together," he says. "Do you feel it? I do. Every moment with you confirms it. I cannot waste another day pretending otherwise."

The ring catches the light again, a miniature sun. I think of security, of never again holding my breath at the grocery checkout. I think of a house where the radiators work, where the girls have their own rooms, where I don't wake at 3 a.m. counting what's left in my account. Most of all, I think of being wanted. Not tolerated. Wanted.

"Yes," I hear myself whisper. My voice doesn't sound like mine. It's thinner and higher than usual, like it slipped free of me before I could test it.

"Yes?" His smile unfurls slowly, triumphant and tender all at once. He slides the ring onto my finger with careful reverence, as though crowning me. "You've made me the happiest man alive."

The diners at the tables nearby clap softly, polite applause for a moment they've only half-witnessed. The sound feels both real and unreal, like applause for a scene in a play. Stuart lifts my hand and presses his lips to the ring, his mouth lingering against the stone.

"We are one now," he murmurs. "Forever."

Rachel's voice flickers again in the back of my mind. Too fast, Ellen. But I silence it. I tell myself she doesn't understand. That she hasn't felt what it is to be chosen like this, to be pulled from obscurity into the light of someone's absolute certainty.

I close my fingers around his, clinging to the hope that maybe, just maybe, I've found what I've been searching for all along. Security. Safety. A promise of a future. I don't dare let myself wonder what the price will be.

4

The church looks like it was carved from the same winter that's drifting down outside. Heavy stone walls, tall arched windows lined with flickers of candlelight, pews that creak when the guests shift in them. Snow dusts the shoulders of the coats hung in the entryway. It should feel holy, like the start of something sacred. Instead, it feels overly staged. Like stepping into a play where everyone already knows their place, and I'm the only one who hasn't memorized the lines.

I stand at the head of the aisle with the satin bouquet Rachel thrust into my hands. My fingers ache from holding it tightly. The candles blur at the edges as if the wax-smoke has seeped into my eyes. The music swells, organ pipes sighing in perfect order, but the moment doesn't feel like mine.

Stuart waits at the altar, steady as a statue. He looks carved for this, broad-shouldered in a suit blacker than the stone behind him. When his eyes catch mine, they don't soften, they sharpen, narrowing with a kind of focus that makes my knees weaken. This is what he wanted. Me, here, now, exactly like this. And that certainty radiates from him like heat.

Amelia and Sophie scatter petals down the aisle before me. Their dresses are cream, their tights sagging a little around the ankles. Sophie beams for a moment, proud of her job, but then clutches the basket tightly and hides behind Amelia's elbow. Amelia, serious as always, walks with perfect concentration, jaw tight, like she understands this is more than a game. When she glances back at me, her brows pinch together in a question she doesn't speak.

Rachel waits in the front pew, her hair gleaming, her lipstick precise. She isn't smiling. Her hands rest folded, but her eyes track every twitch of mine. When I reach the altar and place my hand in Stuart's, Rachel tilts her head the tiniest fraction, and I hear her voice in my mind. Too fast, Ellen. Too fast.

The priest begins. Words about unity, devotion, the sanctity of vows. They wash over me like water running across stone, sinking into nothing. I try to listen, but all I can focus on is the weight of Stuart's hand closing around mine. It's warm, yes, but firm, as though testing my pulse, reminding me he holds it now.

When it's my turn to speak, my mouth is dry. The vows come out thinner than I meant, fragile threads stretched tight. My hands tremble as I slip the ring onto his finger, the gold catching the candlelight in a blinding spark. I think no one notices. But I see Rachel's eyes narrow, and I see Amelia frown, her lips pressed flat.

"Do you, Ellen, take Stuart..."

The priest's words echo through the vaulted ceiling. My name bounces back at me, sounding foreign in his mouth. I hesitate for half a breath and the air swells heavy, waiting. Stuart squeezes my hand, his gaze drilling into mine. I hear Rachel's voice again, urgent this time. Ellen, wait. Think.

"Yes," I say, before the silence can break me. "I do."

The congregation exhales. Stuart smiles, but it's not a

radiant, boyish smile. It's controlled and triumphant. He lifts my hand and kisses the ring he placed there weeks ago, lips pressing to seal the promise like a pact in front of witnesses. Snow drifts against the tall windows, soft and relentless. The candles flicker with the draft of a door opening somewhere at the back. The organ begins again, swelling triumphant, and everyone stands. Stuart leads me down the aisle, his hand covering mine to steer me, guiding me at exactly the pace he's chosen for us.

The guests smile, some clap politely, the rustle of silk and wool filling the church. Faces from his world, not mine, turn toward me, assessing, approving, dismissing. I don't see anyone from my side of life except Rachel and the girls.

Sophie skips now that her job is done, her basket swinging empty. Amelia lingers, walking slower, her eyes darting from me to Stuart, as though trying to solve an equation that doesn't balance. Rachel rises as we pass. She smiles because she must, but her eyes burn with a mix of warning, worry, and defiance. For one heartbeat, I think she'll stand and speak, the way people do in movies, objecting for the bride who can't. But she doesn't. She only watches, her gaze locking on mine until the heavy doors close behind us and the snow swallows us in its cold embrace.

Outside, the bells ring, scattering sound across the city like a net. Stuart pulls me closer under his arm, the fur-lined edge of his coat brushing my cheek.

"You are mine now," he whispers, low enough that only I hear.

My throat tightens. I tell myself the words are romantic, protective, exactly what a husband should say on his wedding day. I silence the unease blooming in my chest, bury Rachel's warning under the swell of organ music still ringing in my ears. I lean into him as the bells toll again, convincing myself this is safety. That this is the beginning of the life I've been waiting for.

But somewhere deep down, I know Rachel is right. This is far too fast.

~

The car waits like a shadow outside the church. Black paint and black glass, idling low and steady. It gleams under the weak lamps as though it's been polished just for this night. The snow falls in a constant sift that quiets the street, swallowing the last of the bells.

I think we'll linger, wave to the few guests braving the cold, maybe let the girls throw one last handful of petals before we leave. But Stuart takes my arm, guiding me firmly down the stone steps. His pace is brisk, final, as if we're fugitives slipping away instead of a bride and groom being celebrated.

Rachel steps forward, her scarf pulled tight around her throat, snow caught in the dark of her lashes. She reaches for me, just a simple touch of farewell, but Stuart's voice cuts the air before she can speak.

"She belongs with me now."

He says it smoothly, without heat, like a fact no one should contest. His hand covers mine, pressing it closer to his side. Rachel's eyes flash, sharp as flint, but she doesn't argue. She only looks at me, hard, as though trying to brand a message straight onto my skin. And I hear what she's saying. I'm here. Remember that. Don't forget.

I nod a tiny, almost imperceptible acknowledgement, but the car door is already opening behind me. Stuart ushers me in with the efficiency of someone closing a deal. Amelia and Sophie are bundled in coats in the back, their flower baskets abandoned on the steps of the church. The driver closes the door with a heavy thump, sealing us into leather and silence.

The engine hums and the car rolls forward. And just like

that, Boston falls behind. The city lights dissolve into gray streaks, then vanish altogether. Snow gathers thick on the highway, flurrying sideways in the wind. Our headlights carve a tunnel ahead of us, leaving nothing visible beyond that narrow beam. I rest my hand on my lap, staring at the ring. It catches the faint glow from the dashboard, blinding me with its insistence. Not long ago, it was pressed onto my finger in front of witnesses. Now it feels heavier, like it has almost fused to the bone.

"Drummond Lodge awaits," Stuart says softly beside me. His voice fills the car the way the snow fills the night. "A proper beginning. Not endless receptions or tedious speeches. It'll be a homecoming."

"Aren't honeymoons supposed to be beaches and cocktails?" I murmur, half joking, half testing.

"Beaches are for those who need distraction," he says. "We need only truth. And the Lodge will give us that."

The Lodge. He's spoken of it so often. His family estate tucked deep in the Adirondacks, the place where his mother raised him, and where every stone and beam is weighted with memory. I've never seen it, only glimpsed it through the devotion in his voice, and the way he paints it. A place that sounds less like a house than a shrine.

I press my forehead lightly to the cold glass, watching the snow ribbon past. Somewhere behind us, I imagine Rachel standing under the lamps, scarf tight, face lifted into the storm. The image clings, makes my throat ache. The girls whisper in the back seat.

"Where are we going?" Amelia's voice is low and tight.

"To Daddy's," Sophie suggests, though she doesn't sound convinced.

Amelia shakes her head. "No. Not Daddy's." Then louder, directed to me. "Mom?"

I turn, forcing a smile. "We're going to the mountains. A new house."

Her brows knit. "Forever?"

I hesitate. The word sticks. Stuart answers for me.

"Yes," he says firmly. "Forever."

"But what about Daddy?"

Stuart bristles.

"I'm your Daddy, now."

My heart jumps. I had arranged with Thomas that I'd keep the girls with us for a couple of weeks. But I'd also promised him that this would change nothing for him and the girls. Now, I see I was wrong to promise that. Silence fills the back seat. Sophie curls into Amelia's side, their hands knotting together. I watch their reflection in the glass, two small shapes, clinging to each other as the dark swallows the world beyond.

The storm worsens as we leave the highway. The car climbs narrower roads, with heavy snow piling high at their shoulders. Pines lean over us, their branches bowing heavy with white. The headlights slice through them, catching flashes of eyeshine, deer maybe, or wolves.

I shift in my seat, feeling restless. My whole body hums with the realization of how quickly my life has spun. A month ago, I was scraping peanut butter from the counter, counting out lunch money, pretending I wasn't terrified of the rent. Tonight, I am in a car with a man who wears certainty like a second skin, with a ring burning my finger, and my daughters asleep in the back, being carried into a future I can't picture.

I should feel relief. I should feel saved. But under the relief there's a whisper of unease that even the warmth of the car can't melt. Stuart reaches over, touches my chin, tilting it up.

"Don't look down," he murmurs. "You're mine now. You must look the world in the eye."

I nod, because it's easier than disagreeing, easier than admitting that sometimes all I want is to look away. His thumb lingers at my jaw, then withdraws. He turns back to the window, eyes on the darkness.

"Isobel loved the snow most at night," he says. "She used to take me walking in storms like this, telling me the cold makes the air honest. That the snow hides everything false."

There she is again. Always just beneath the surface. His mother's shadow is traveling with us, even now. I tell myself it's love. That he speaks of her the way I speak of Amelia and Sophie. Devotion, not obsession. The car jostles over a drift, the tires spinning before catching again. Sophie stirs, mutters, then curls tighter against Amelia.

"Are we close?" I ask, voice thinner than I intend.

"Closer with every mile," Stuart says, and his tone is threaded with something almost reverent. "You'll see. The Lodge isn't just a house. It's all the world we need. It's a place where you can finally stop running."

I glance back at the girls, at Amelia's watchful eyes glinting in the dark. She doesn't believe him. I'm not sure I do either. But I keep my silence, the snow pounding against the glass, the road unspooling into white nothingness ahead.

Hours blur. The hum of the engine, the steady sweep of wipers, the hypnotic rush of flakes in the headlights, all of it numbs me. My hand keeps finding the ring, turning it, testing its weight. At some point, I drift into half-sleep, only to jolt awake when the car slows. Stuart's hand is already on my knee, steadying, anchoring.

"Almost there now," he says, as though I asked.

The girls are both asleep now, their heads tipped together. I want to scoop them close, tuck them into my side, shield them from everything unknown waiting beyond the dark. Instead, I sit still, my throat tight, the snow pressing harder on the roof. Because I want to believe. And because turning back now would mean admitting I've walked willingly into something I can't escape.

5

The car crunches to a halt on gravel that glitters with ice. For a long moment, no one moves. The engine ticks, the storm hushes, and then I see Drummond Lodge rising from the snow like something carved out of myth. It isn't a house, it's a fortress dressed as one. Stone walls climb high, their edges blurred by snowdrifts, and timber beams cut black against the white sky. Lanterns burn in wrought-iron sconces along the entry, casting weak circles of gold that slide across the ice. The forest crowds close on every side, towering pines with branches heavy and bent, as though bowing toward the house in some grim allegiance.

I catch my breath. For a second, awe outweighs unease. I've never seen anything like it. My childhood was cramped apartments, peeling paint, radiators clanking at midnight. Even with Thomas, our houses were modest and practical. This is another world. But the silence presses hard. There's no traffic hum, no neighbor's television, no city sigh. Only the moan of the wind through the trees, the snow settling silently, and the Lodge itself, looming, waiting.

"Home," Stuart murmurs. His voice carries something reverent, almost holy.

The girls stir awake in the back. Sophie blinks, her small face pale against her scarf.

"It's so big," she whispers. Amelia just stares, jaw tight, her hands still clasped around Sophie's like she's bracing for something painful.

Stuart opens the door, his boots crunching on ice.

"Come," he says, already circling the car. "See where we belong."

I gather the girls, ushering them out into the cold. The air here bites sharper than in Boston, both cleaner and more brutal at once. Sophie shivers, burying her face against my coat. Amelia doesn't complain, but her eyes flick from the trees to the windows to the heavy front door, cataloguing everything, as if she already knows this isn't just a place to live, it's a place to survive.

The door opens before we reach it. A figure stands framed in the lantern light. Mrs. Lennox. I know her name because Stuart mentioned her on the drive, in passing.

"The housekeeper's been there longer than anyone. She'll see to everything."

Even forewarned, I wasn't prepared for the sight of her. She's in her sixties, wiry, her posture iron-straight despite the weight of the years. Her hair is pulled so tightly into a knot that it shines under the light. Her dress is dark, plain, and old-fashioned in a way that makes her look more like part of the house than its keeper. And her eyes are sharp gray, and unflinching. They fix on me first, then the girls. They linger, not warmly, but with something heavier. Pity. It rattles me more than outright hostility would.

"Mr. Drummond," she says. Her voice is crisp, carrying the

clipped cadence of someone who doesn't waste words. "The rooms are ready."

"Good," Stuart says. He places his hand on my back, steering me forward as though I need prompting. "This is Ellen. And my daughters, Amelia and Sophie."

The words land with a thud in the snow between us. My daughters. But he says it with ownership, not acknowledgment.

Mrs. Lennox dips her chin in a gesture that isn't quite a bow.

"Welcome." But her eyes don't match her voice. They rest on me, steady but hooded, and again there's that flicker of pity that makes my stomach tighten. I force a smile, though my lips tremble in the cold.

"Thank you."

The girls press against me as we cross the threshold. The heavy door closes behind us with a sound like a vault sealing.

Inside, the Lodge is vast and shadowed, the air carrying that peculiar weight of places shut up for a long time, and suddenly opened again. A cavernous hall stretches ahead, timber beams arching overhead like ribs. Rugs muted with age sprawl across the floor, their patterns dulled by decades of feet. A fire roars in a stone hearth taller than any man, its flames leaping, its heat struggling to reach the edges of the room.

Paintings line the walls. Portraits mostly. Serious men, pale women, all with the same austere jaw, the same Drummond eyes. Their gazes follow us, unblinking, as though measuring whether we're worthy to pass. The girls cling tighter.

"It smells old," Sophie whispers.

She isn't wrong. Smoke, polish, dust, and age lace the air.

"Grand, isn't it?" Stuart's voice fills the hall. His boots echo on the stone as he strides forward. "Every stone placed by hand. Every beam cut from the forest. My mother made certain it would outlast us all."

He stops before the fire, spreading his arms as though

embracing it. The light gilds his face, throwing his features into sharp relief.

"This is where we begin, Ellen. You and I. And the girls."

I nod, though my throat feels dry. The grandeur is overwhelming, yes, but there's no softness here either. No sense of welcome. Just scale and weight. Mrs. Lennox watches me from the side, her hands hanging limply at her waist. She hasn't moved since we entered. When I glance her way, she doesn't look away, and her eyes pin me again, gray and relentless. That pity sharpens into a warning, maybe, though unspoken.

Sophie tugs at my coat.

"I want to go home," she whispers.

"We are home," Stuart says firmly, though she wasn't speaking to him. His voice carries across the hall, echoing against stone. "You'll learn to love it."

Amelia's face hardens. She says nothing, but her small jaw sets in that way I recognize as her silent rebellion, her refusal to yield. I kneel, smoothing Sophie's hair, kissing the crown of her head.

"We'll make it ours," I murmur, though the words taste hollow.

Behind me, the fire cracks, the portraits watch, and Mrs. Lennox's gray eyes don't blink. The Lodge feels ready to swallow us whole.

The stairs groan under our weight as we climb, each step a hollow drumbeat in the vast silence. The girls are left below with Mrs. Lennox. Amelia gave me a look I'll never forget, fully fierce and reluctant, before taking Sophie's hand. Stuart didn't ask if I wanted them to come along, he simply steered me upward with a hand at my shoulder, decisive, like always.

The corridor stretches long and dim, lined with doors that look too tall and heavy for ordinary use. The rugs here are thick enough to swallow sound, and only the creak of wood beneath tells me this house is real. Stuart walks ahead, past muted wall sconces whose glow spills in arcs over polished banisters and carved panels.

At last, he stops before a door near the end of the hall. The brass handle gleams as if it's been polished daily, though I can't imagine who would bother in a place this enormous. Stuart pushes the door open, and the corridor light leaps into the room. The Blue Suite.

I step inside and feel as though I've trespassed. The walls are papered in a rich indigo patterned with lilies. Heavy curtains of velvet, the same deep blue, hang from tall windows, their folds falling in perfect symmetry. The bed is vast, draped with a quilt embroidered with silver thread that catches the lantern's glow. A faint, powdery scent lingers in the air, as though someone recently spilled a bottle of perfume. Nothing here feels lived in. It feels kept and preserved. A room sealed away from time.

I move to the dresser. The surface is bare, but when I draw a finger along the edge of the mirror, dust doesn't cling. Someone has been tending this place and protecting it from the elements. Stuart turns to me.

"This will be your room."

I blink at him. "Mine?"

He nods. "The Blue Suite. My mother's room."

I stop breathing for a moment. The words carry weight.

"Stuart..." I swallow, forcing gentleness into my voice. "Are you sure? Maybe one of the other rooms would be..."

He cuts me off, his tone sharp enough to slice.

"No. It has to be this one."

I glance around again, trying to calm the prickle at the back of my neck. The bed is perfectly made, the curtains are rigid, the air ominously still. It's like stepping into a shrine, not a bedroom.

"I don't want to disturb anything," I say carefully. "It feels... like it still belongs to her."

He crosses the room in two strides, taking my shoulders in his hands. His grip is firm, almost bruising. His eyes blaze in the dim light.

"She would have wanted you here. Do you understand? She would have wanted it."

The intensity in his voice freezes me. I nod quickly, though unease pools in my stomach.

"Of course. If you're sure."

His hands soften, sliding down my arms.

"You'll grow to love it," he says, quieter now, almost tender. "The color, the silence, the way the moonlight falls on the floor in winter. She always said the Blue Suite teaches patience. Endurance." His eyes catch mine and hold. "You need only surrender to it."

The words unsettle me, though I tell myself it's the strangeness of a new place, the residue of grief in him. To him, this room is sacred. But to me, it feels suffocating. I turn to the window, pulling the curtain aside. Outside, the forest presses close, black trunks and snow-laden branches hemming the Lodge in. No lights anywhere, not a single house, not even the sweep of a road. Just endless trees, silent and watching.

Behind me, Stuart's reflection fills the mirror, tall and dark. His gaze is on me, not the room. Not the house or his memories, but on me. I let the curtain fall back, blocking out the forest.

"It's beautiful," I manage, though the word sounds thin in the heavy air.

"Yes," he says, as though sealing the decision. "Beautiful. And yours now."

I touch the quilt, tracing the stitched lilies, and feel the faintest shiver climb my spine. The embroidery is fine and delicate, but worn smooth in places, as though someone's hands once lingered here night after night. A ghost of habit.

I wonder if Isobel ever lay awake here, staring at the same ceiling, listening to the forest shift against the windows. I wonder if she felt trapped, too. Stuart's arm comes around my waist. His lips brush my hair.

"You will honor her," he murmurs. "By living here. By filling this room again."

The weight of his certainty presses down on me. I smile because I must, because resistance would sour the air between us. But inside, a quiet voice whispers what I don't dare say aloud. This isn't a gift. It's a command and a penalty. The Blue Suite claims me. Its silence is thick, patient. And somewhere, in the dark corners, I swear I can feel Isobel watching.

6

The first morning in the Lodge feels like waking inside a cave. Light does come with morning, but it seeps rather than shines. The heavy curtains drink most of it, leaving only a dull gray glow across the long breakfast table. The fire burns low, its smoke catching in my throat. Somewhere deeper in the house, pipes groan, carrying water through the veins of the stone.

At breakfast, Mrs. Lennox lays out dishes with the precision of a clockmaker. Porridge, toast, a tray of ripe fruit that couldn't have grown anywhere near these mountains. She places each item in silence, her lips pressed thin, her eyes never quite lifting.

Sophie climbs onto her chair beside me, her legs swinging.

"It smells funny here," she whispers, wrinkling her nose. I hush her gently, smoothing her hair. Amelia sits straighter, quiet but watchful, as if she's already learned that too much noise here feels dangerous. Stuart takes his place at the head of the table. He looks perfectly at home, like the carved chair was made for him, which it probably was. He rests his napkin in his lap, then glances at me.

"Ellen." He nods toward my fork. "The handle should rest

against the base of your finger, not float between them. It shows confidence."

I blink, adjusting automatically, feeling my cheeks warming at the rebuke.

"Right," I murmur.

He smiles, approving, as though I've passed a test.

Sophie chatters about the snow outside, about how the branches looked like hands when she peeked through the window. She mimics them with her little fingers curling. I laugh softly, glad for a moment of childish lightness. But Stuart's gaze sharpens.

"Sophie," he says gently, but there's iron under it. "Don't wave your hands over the table. It's sloppy. Sit up nice and still."

Her hands freeze mid-air. She lowers them slowly, biting her lip.

"She's only five," I begin carefully.

"And five is old enough to learn," he interrupts, voice smooth. He turns to Amelia. "You sit well. Upright, attentive. That's how a young lady ought to present herself."

Amelia's cheeks flush. She stiffens her back even more, eyes down. The porridge cools in my bowl and my appetite drains away. I try to smile, to keep the mood light, but my hands tremble faintly as I lift my spoon. Stuart notices. He always notices. His hand closes over mine, steadying the spoon.

"There," he says softly, almost tender. "See how easy it is, when someone guides you?"

The words should comfort but, they land like a chain slipped around my wrist. Across the table, Mrs. Lennox stands motionless, her hands folded now, her gaze fixed on the far wall. She doesn't speak, doesn't interfere. But I feel her awareness, like she's cataloguing every correction, every silence, every flinch. When I meet her eyes, briefly, she looks away as though she's afraid to be drawn into anything.

Sophie pushes her porridge aside, her shoulders hunching. Amelia places a steadying hand on her sister's knee beneath the table. I see it, though Stuart does not. I try to start conversation.

"The forest is beautiful," I say, forcing brightness. "The girls could explore today, maybe near the gardens?"

Stuart shakes his head immediately.

"Not until they understand boundaries. The woods are vast. It's easy to lose yourself if you're careless."

"They wouldn't be alone," I say quickly. "I'd go with them."

His smile is faint, indulgent. "In time. For now, let them learn the house. There is more than enough to discover inside these walls."

Inside these walls. The phrase makes my skin crawl. Breakfast drags on. Stuart critiques the way Amelia holds her spoon, the angle of my wrist when I pour milk. Each comment is wrapped in civility, but the edges are sharp.

"Refinement," he calls it. "Teaching you how to belong."

By the time Mrs. Lennox clears the dishes, my nerves are frayed raw. I kiss the girls' heads, sending them to the hearth with their dolls, and follow Stuart into the hall. Behind us, Mrs. Lennox moves like a shadow, collecting plates. She doesn't meet my eye again, but I can feel what she won't say. She knows what's happening here. She's seen this before.

The Lodge falls quiet. Even the children's laughter seems swallowed by its walls. And as I trail after Stuart's long stride, I wonder how long it will be before silence becomes the only language we're allowed to speak.

The study is the warmest room in the lodge, but warmth here feels more like an order than a comfort. The fire throws a steady glow over shelves that stretch from floor to ceiling, each lined with heavy spines of cracked leather, embossed with gilt lettering dulled by time. Stuart's paintings lean against the walls in carefully arranged groups, some framed, some raw canvas stretched over wood. They smell faintly of linseed oil, the sharpness of which cuts through the woody scent of the fire.

It should feel safe, even cozy, but it feels empty. The windows are shuttered, and the curtains in front of them are heavy velvet falling in thick folds, and the fire's light stops just short of the corners where the shadows are so deep, they seem to breathe.

Stuart gestures to the armchair opposite his desk.

"Sit."

I obey, smoothing my skirt as I lower myself. My hands are cold despite the heat of the room. He remains standing, one arm braced against the mantel, his profile gilded by flame. He looks every inch the portrait of authority. Like a figure belonging in one of these heavy frames, or someone you'd find in a history book.

"This room," he says. "Is the heart of the lodge. My father ruled from here. My mother..." He pauses, his jaw tightening. "She preserved it. And now, Ellen, you and I will begin here. Everything we decide, everything we do, will echo outward through this house."

I nod, unsure what he expects me to say. He crosses to his desk, fingers gliding across the polished surface.

"There are rules here, which you and the girls must obey. They're not arbitrary or cruel. They're in place to protect us, and preserve what is sacred." His eyes flick to me. "You understand the value of rules. A household cannot survive chaos."

I think of Amelia, precise with her homework, and Sophie, who resists almost every decision. I think of the way my old apartment ran on improvisation, how structure was something I faked more than enforced.

"Yes," I murmur. "Rules matter."

"Good." He smiles faintly, pleased. "Then hear mine."

He begins pacing slowly, hands clasped behind his back.

"Outside contact must be limited. The world beyond these trees corrupts, distracts. People meddle, pry, and destroy what they envy. Here, we are insulated. We can remain untouched."

My mouth opens, instinctively, to protest, to say that we need to be part of the world, but I catch his eyes and falter.

"You mean... no letters? Phone calls? Emails?"

His smile doesn't shift. "You won't need them. If something is essential, it can be arranged. But otherwise... no. We don't need others. We are sufficient for each other."

I swallow. Rachel's face flares in my mind, her sharp eyes, her fierce warnings. Too fast, Ellen. I imagine her dialing me, leaving a message that will never reach me now.

"But the girls," I say softly. "Their friends, their teachers, Thomas..."

"They will adapt," he interrupts. "Children thrive in order, not distraction. The lodge will be their school and their sanctuary."

The fire pops. Sophie's laugh echoes faintly from somewhere downstairs, muffled by stone. The sound feels fragile, already at risk of being swallowed. He stops pacing, facing me squarely now.

"You must also respect the sanctity of this house. Every room has history and every wall breathes memory. It is not a place to be altered on a whim, and it doesn't welcome intrusion. Do you understand?"

I nod quickly, though the Blue Suite flashes in my mind, with its powdery perfume still clinging to the air, and the sense of another woman's presence pressing against me. I want to say that I don't want to live in a shrine. But his gaze pins me, steady and insistent, and I know which answer is acceptable.

"Yes. I understand."

His shoulders ease, satisfied. "Good. Then one last thing."

He comes closer, perching on the edge of the desk directly across from me. His knees nearly touch mine. His voice lowers, intimate, as if confiding a secret.

"You must give yourself fully to family life here. No distractions. No old ambitions clinging to your mind. You will care for the girls, of course. You will be the heart. And I..." He touches his chest with his fingertips. "I will be the head. Together, complete."

The words are beautiful in shape but heavy in weight. You will, not would you, not could you. Commands disguised as devotion. I nod again, because what else can I do? His hand brushes my cheek, tender but possessive.

"You'll see. Simplicity suits you. The world has bruised you, but here you will heal."

My throat tightens. I want to believe him. I want to believe safety lives within these walls. But under his touch, I feel the faintest chill, like the walls aren't sheltering me at all, but closing in.

Later, he summons Mrs. Lennox into the study. She glides in silently, hands clasped. Her expression is neutral, her eyes dim. She doesn't look at me, only at Stuart.

"I need to fetch something from the cellar," Stuart says. "Stay here with Ellen."

It feels strangely unnecessary. I don't need company while he leaves the room. But the way he says it, the formality of it, makes it clear this isn't about my comfort or reassurance. It's a test. Mrs. Lennox inclines her head.

"Of course."

He disappears into the corridor, his footsteps already fading as the study door clicks shut. Silence swells. Mrs. Lennox stands by the window, her profile stern, hands still clasped. I shift in my chair, suddenly aware of the fire's heat, and the stifling closeness of the room. I clear my throat.

"It's…a beautiful house."

Her eyes flick to me, then away again. "It has stood a long time."

The answer is clipped, cautious. She doesn't invite more. I try again.

"You must know it better than anyone."

Her mouth tightens. She doesn't speak. I lean forward, lowering my voice.

"Do you like it here?"

This time, her eyes meet mine fully. For a fraction of a second, I see the same pity I glimpsed when we first arrived, the shadow of something she won't say, but then she looks away, her voice sharp as she replies.

"My place is to serve, not enjoy."

I sit back, chastened. Silence swallows us again. The fire crackles, the shadows shift. When Stuart returns, carrying nothing, his eyes sweep the room as if measuring the air. He looks at Mrs. Lennox first.

"You may go."

She nods, slipping out without a word. Then he turns to me.

"What did you talk about?"

The question is soft, almost casual, but my stomach drops.

"Nothing much. The house."

His eyes narrow. "Exactly what words?"

I falter. "I said it was beautiful. She said… it had stood a long time."

"And?" His gaze sharpens, a scalpel poised.

"I asked if she liked it here. She said her place was to serve."

The silence after my confession is heavier than stone. Then, slowly, his expression softens. He crosses the room, kneels before me, takes my hands in his.

"You must be careful," he says gently. "Words matter. Curiosity can be dangerous. Mrs. Lennox is loyal, but I don't want you distracted by her ideas, or anyone else's. You have me. That is enough." His grip tightens on my hands. "Do you understand?"

I nod quickly, relief and unease tangling in my chest.

"Good." He kisses my knuckles, lingering, his eyes locked on mine. "That's why I love you. You listen. You yield. You belong."

I want to feel cherished. I want to feel safe. And for a moment, I almost do. His intensity has a gravity that pulls me in, makes the rest of the world blur. But his words echo in my mind long after he lets go. You yield. We don't need others. They circle like chains, invisible but tightening.

7

The snow falls so heavily it blankets sound. From the Blue Suite's tall windows, I watch it sift down in thick, endless waves, piling against the glass. The forest outside is nearly gone, smudged into whiteness, as though the world has been swallowed whole. Even the girls' laughter from down the hall reaches me only faintly, muffled, like voices underwater.

It's the first time since arriving that I've been left alone. Stuart is with Mrs. Lennox in the study. The girls are exploring the wide staircases, Sophie clinging to Amelia's hand, both of them half curious, half wary. I tell myself this is the moment to unpack, to begin making this room my own. I kneel by the trunk at the foot of the bed, setting my suitcase beside it. My fingers hover at the latch, my chest tight. The Blue Suite doesn't feel like mine, no matter what Stuart insists. The air itself resists me. It holds a sweetness that isn't natural, its perfume lingering long after it should have faded, clinging to the curtains, the quilt, even the wood.

I pull open the first drawer of the tall dresser. And freeze. Silk spills out in muted waves of cream and pale blue, folded perfectly. Gowns, delicate and old, their hems stitched with lace yellowed by age. They lie as if waiting for someone to lift them out, shake them free, and slip them back on. A faint perfume rises as the fabric shifts of violets and lavender, but heavy and cloying.

I open another drawer to find more gowns, more slips, stockings still folded around cardboard. Behind them, tucked at the back, is a small box of perfume bottles. Their glass stoppers gleam, some of the bottles are cloudy with residue, some still full, the liquid inside turned the color of amber. When I uncork one, the scent slams into me, like powder and rot, both at once. I close it quickly, my stomach twisting.

The third drawer resists, sticking slightly before sliding open. Inside are stacks of letters, tied with faded ribbon. The envelopes are brittle, their edges curled, and some of the ink is blurred. I don't touch them. I don't feel that I can. The sight alone is enough. Isobel. Her presence hums through the room. It isn't memory and it isn't even grief. It's preservation. She has been kept here, in her dresses, her perfumes, her words, like a pressed flower under glass. Stuart hasn't let her go. He's built her a shrine and placed me inside it to fill the space she's left vacant.

I let the drawer fall shut with a thud and feel my heart hammering in my throat as the door creaks open. I startle, turning, half-afraid it's Stuart. But it's Amelia, standing in the doorway, her small face pale in the dim light. She wrinkles her nose, stepping inside cautiously.

"It smells funny in here."

I force a smile. "Old houses always do. The wood, the fabrics, they keep the air different."

She drifts toward the dresser, glancing at the curtains, the heavy quilt. Her eyes are sharp.

"Wasn't this his mom's room?"

The question lands like a stone in my stomach.

"Yes," I say, quickly. Then softer, "But it's mine now."

Amelia studies me, her brow furrowed. She doesn't believe me. I can see it in the way her lips press together, the way her eyes flick toward the drawers I didn't close tightly enough. She smells the perfume just as strongly, and she feels the weight of someone else still here. She knows just as well as I do that it's a weight I can neither lift nor replace. Sophie would have asked a hundred questions. Amelia doesn't. She just stands there, quiet, and that silence feels louder than words. I cross to her, smoothing her hair.

"It'll feel more like ours once we've settled in," I whisper. "Give it time."

She nods, but her body is stiff, and her trust is hesitant. She slips away a moment later, leaving me alone again in the suffocating Blue Suite. I stand in the middle of the room, my pulse drumming, and realize that I am not just living in another woman's house. I am living in her shadow. And shadows can be hard to escape.

~

The lodge is quiet in the late afternoon. Heavy snow still presses against the windows, muting the outside world into oppressive blankness. Inside, only the fire downstairs crackles, a dull heartbeat in a house that seems otherwise asleep. I should be resting, or unpacking properly, or coaxing the girls into games that make the place feel less alien to all of us. But something pulls me back to the dresser.

The top drawer sits slightly ajar from earlier, as if the gowns inside are leaning forward, waiting for me to lift them out. My eyes drift to the rear of the drawer, to a small jewelry box I hadn't noticed before. It's tucked in the corner, half-hidden beneath a silk shawl.

The box is wooden, dark walnut, the surface carved with tiny vines. Dust settles in the grooves, but the clasp gleams faintly, polished by years of use. My breath catches. This doesn't look like part of the display, like the untouched gowns and folded stockings. This looks personal. A thing someone would open daily, touch, cherish, and keep hidden from prying eyes.

It's Isobel's, of course. I know it before I even touch it. I glance at the door, listening for footfall. The hall is still. The house is vast. Stuart is surely with Mrs. Lennox in the study again, discussing the order of the household, or instructing her on some unseen detail. The girls are playing downstairs, I can just barely hear Sophie's sing-song voice drifting up when the silence shifts.

It feels safe to look, just for a moment. My fingers brush the lid. The wood is smooth, warmer than I imagined. I undo the clasp with a faint click. The sound seems loud, like it might echo down the corridor. I wait, listening again, ready to spring it shut and shove it to the back of the drawer. But no sound comes.

I slowly lift the lid. Inside, velvet the color of dusk cradles a scattering of jewelry. Pearls, yellowed slightly with age. A brooch inlaid with sapphires. A ring with a thin band worn nearly smooth. And a delicate chain, its pendant a teardrop of blue glass, no bigger than the nail of my thumb. I lift the chain carefully. The pendant sways, catching the dim light, throwing a blue spark across the quilt. It's lovely, but there's something mournful about it too, like it belongs more to a coffin than a throat.

I wonder if Stuart's mother wore it often. If she touched it absentmindedly while looking out the same window I've looked through, watching the forest shift against the snow. Did she feel trapped here, too? Did she dream of leaving?

A floorboard creaks behind me and my stomach plunges. I turn, with the pendant still in my hand, to find Stuart standing in the doorway, his figure framed by the dim hall. His face is dark, the light from the landing casting half of it in shadow. For a moment, neither of us speaks. Then his voice, low and sharp.

"You mustn't disturb her things."

The words crack through the air. Not loud. Not shouted. But terribly final. I freeze, the pendant swinging faintly between my fingers. My mouth goes dry.

"I...I 'm sorry. I was only..."

"Looking?" His eyes narrow. He steps into the room, the weight of his boots sinking into the rug. "Prying?"

Heat burns my cheeks. "No. I didn't mean. I was looking for somewhere to unpack my things. It was just there, and I..."

He stops close enough that I can smell the faint trace of paint on him, linseed and turpentine. His gaze drops to the pendant, then back to my face. His jaw is clenched, a muscle ticking.

"She was so delicate," he says, his voice low, taut. "Everything she touched is delicate. It must be preserved. That way Do you understand?"

I nod quickly, heart pounding. "Yes. I understand. I didn't mean to..."

He plucks the pendant from my hand with a swift motion, as if rescuing it from danger. He lays it back in the box with exaggerated care, closes the lid, and fastens the clasp. His hands linger on it for a moment, smoothing the surface like one might soothe a child. And then he places it on the dresser top with a small pat on its lid.

The silence between us thickens, suffocating. I want to move, but I'm fixed to the spot, waiting for his next move. Then, just as quickly, his expression shifts. His shoulders soften. He reaches for my hand, lifting it to his lips. The kiss is slow, deliberate, and his eyes never leave mine.

"You are my wife now," he says gently, though something

colder glints behind his words. "You don't need trinkets from the past. And you don't need to be anyone else. You have me."

His mouth lingers on my skin. To anyone else, it might look tender. But his linger with a weight that makes my stomach twist, as though he is both loving and measuring me, ensuring I will not cross some invisible line again.

I whisper, "Of course."

His thumb strokes the back of my hand once, then releases it. He straightens, his voice returning to that calm certainty that always makes me feel both reassured and trapped.

"There are things in this house that are sacred," he says. "Things you must not disturb. You'll learn which. And when you do, you'll see that obedience is not weakness, it is strength."

I nod again, quickly. My throat feels tight, as though the air itself has hardened. He studies me for a long moment, then finally smiles, softening once more. He brushes a stray hair from my face, the gesture intimate, almost tender.

"You'll grow to love this room," he murmurs. "She would have wanted it."

Then, he leaves me standing there, the jewelry box gleaming but shut, my hands trembling. The door closes softly behind him and the silence that remains is louder than anything he said.

I sit on the edge of the bed, my pulse still racing. The Blue Suite feels smaller now, its velvet curtains closing tighter around me. I can't shake the image of his face when he caught me. His features revealed the hardness of his fury as he pressed it under control. He hadn't shouted. That would have been easier, maybe. Instead, he wielded silence, and quiet precision. His displeasure was sharper because it was so quiet.

I look at the jewelry box again. It sits where he left it, ordinary and still. But now it feels like a warning, not a curiosity. A forbidden thing that will cause more harm than good. The perfume in the air seems stronger suddenly, even more cloying, as if Isobel herself is pressing closer, and whispering. You don't belong here.

The girls' laughter drifts faintly from downstairs again. Sophie's giggle, Amelia's firmer voice. I cling to the sound of them, grounding myself. But even that sound feels fragile, as though the lodge is already swallowing it, already teaching them silence.

I tell myself it was nothing but a misunderstanding. He was protective, not cruel. He only wants to preserve what mattered to his mother. That's love, isn't it? That's devotion. But deep down, I know better. His reaction wasn't about jewelry, it was about control. And he's left the box here deliberately, in plain sight, to tempt me, taunt me, and test me.

8

The parlor smells faintly of polish and smoke, the air thick with the residue of years of fires burned low in the grate. Heavy curtains swallow most of the daylight, leaving the room hushed and dim. It's one of the smaller spaces in the Lodge, or at least one of the few that doesn't make me feel like a child wandering through a cathedral. The shelves here are lined with books in cracked leather, their titles faded to ghosts, and a pair of armchairs sit angled toward the fire as if still waiting for occupants who never returned.

In the far corner, a polished mahogany desk holds a single object. A simple telephone. Its black receiver gleams against the dark wood. The cord, stiff with age, curls in a neat loop. It looks ordinary, if slightly old fashioned. It looks dependable. And for a moment, just seeing it steadies me. There is a connection to the outside world, after all.

I cross the rug and pick up the receiver, pressing it to my ear. Silence. Then, faintly, a crackle. A distant hum, like wind in a tunnel. I frown, jiggling the hook.

"Come on..."

A burst of static hisses in my ear, sharp enough to make me

flinch. Then nothing. No dial tone. No further hiss. Nothing. I press the receiver harder, as though force might coax sound through the line.

"Please," I whisper, ridiculous, pleading with a machine. "Just work."

Behind me, the door creaks. I whirl, my heart thumping. Mrs. Lennox stands in the doorway, her figure stiff against the dim hall beyond. Her hands are folded, as always. She regards me for a long moment before speaking, her voice low and matter-of-fact.

"The phones are often unreliable this far out."

My cheeks flush, as if she's caught me doing something illicit. I lower the receiver slowly, setting it back into its cradle with a muted click.

"It's dead," I say, quickly.

She steps into the room, her shoes soundless on the rug. "They go down in storms. Lines freeze, wires snap." Her eyes flick to the window, where snow still drifts past in thick veils. "Sometimes they're out for days."

Days. The word lodges in my chest. I try to smile, to cover the tightening in my throat.

"I was just trying to call a friend in Boston. To let her know we'd arrived safely."

Mrs. Lennox's gaze lingers on me, gray and heavy. Then she nods once, brisk, and smooths her skirt.

"You won't need to trouble yourself. If it's important, Mr. Drummond will see it one."

I open my mouth, but the words shrivel before they leave me. She's already turned back toward the door. Her posture is so rigid it looks painful, her back a line of obedience carved by decades. When she's gone, the room feels even smaller than before, the silence louder. I stare at the phone, black and gleaming on the polished wood. So close, and yet as unreachable as if it were locked in glass.

That evening, I try again. The girls are upstairs, giggling faintly in the room Stuart has set for them. Their laughter is a thread I cling to as I slip back into the parlor. The fire has burned low, embers glowing. The phone sits where I left it, smug in its uselessness. I lift the receiver and hear static again. A long, low sigh in the line, like someone breathing from very far away. But still no dial tone.

"Please," I whisper, though I don't know who I'm asking. Rachel's face rises in my mind, her arched brow, her knowing smirk. If I could just hear her sharp, sarcastic, unflinching voice, it would cut through the fog settling over me. But there's nothing there and no way of reaching her. The silence in the line is not just absence. It feels like a deliberate wall being held up. I set the phone down, my hand trembling.

Later, over supper, I force myself to ask him about it. Like so many other rooms here, the dining hall is cavernous, and the fire struggled to keep up with the size of the room. Shadows climb the walls like restless figures. Stuart sits at the head of the table, carving into a roast Mrs. Lennox has prepared. The girls pick at their plates. Amelia polite but tight-jawed, Sophie yawning into her sleeve. I clear my throat.

"I tried the phone today. It doesn't seem to be working."

Stuart looks up, the carving knife pausing midair.

"Ah." He sets it down carefully. "The lines are unreliable out here. They always have been."

"I wanted to let Rachel know we arrived," I say. My voice sounds thin and defensive.

He smiles faintly, indulgent. "Rachel will assume you're well. She'll hear from you soon enough."

I hesitate. "And if I needed to make a call? For the girls, or..."

His gaze sharpens, though his smile doesn't waver. "You won't need to. Anything essential, I'll handle."

"But..."

He reaches across the table, his hand covering mine. His grip is warm, firm, silencing. "You'll see, my love. Simplicity suits us. The world beyond these trees has only hurt you. Here, you'll never be hurt again."

His thumb strokes my knuckles, tender but possessive. The girls are watch us silently. Sophie's wide eyes flit from his face to mine. Amelia's brow furrows, her lips pressed thin. I force a smile.

"Of course."

His expression eases, and he seems satisfied with my reply. He lifts his glass, his voice rich and final.

"To family. To peace."

I echo the words, but the wine tastes bitter on my tongue, and inside, unease spreads like frost.

Later, as I tuck the girls into bed, Amelia whispers, "Why doesn't the phone work?"

I smooth her hair, avoiding her eyes.

"The snow, maybe. It'll come back on soon."

She watches me, sharp and doubtful. Sophie cuddles close to her sister, already half-asleep, trusting the silence because she must. I kiss them both, linger a moment longer, then slip out into the corridor. The Blue Suite waits down the hall, with its velvet curtains heavy with perfume. But I can't shake the image of the phone. Black, gleaming, silent. Like a mirage. A door that looks open, but isn't.

9

A renewed burst of the storm begins just before supper the next day. By the time Mrs. Lennox calls us to the dining room, the wind has picked up enough to rattle the shutters, and sounds like a constant gnashing against the glass. Snow drives in furious sheets across the tall windows, reducing the world outside to a blur of white and shadow. Inside, the fire in the hearth fights to keep up, its roar swallowed by the howl whistling across the top of the chimney, drawing the flames too fast.

The dining room is long and severe, its carved chairs arranged like soldiers around the vast table. The girls sit across from me, Sophie's feet swinging, Amelia composed but rigid. Stuart presides at the head, knife and fork at the ready. Mrs Lennox delivers a simple meal of lamb, potatoes and steamed vegetables. The smell of meat and rosemary fills the air, but my stomach knots too tightly to be hungry.

Sophie hums softly to herself, trying to make the silence less heavy. Amelia doesn't speak at all. She only watches, her eyes darting between Stuart and me like she's measuring something unseen. I lift my fork, forcing normalcy.

"The storm sounds fierce tonight. It's lucky we're warm in here."

Neither girl answers. Stuart skewers a slice of meat on his fork, studying it, before placing it in his mouth, chewing cautiously. His movements are precise, deliberate, almost ceremonial.

Then, without warning, Amelia sets her fork down with a sharp clink. Her voice slices through the room, steady but trembling at the edges.

"I don't like it here. I want to go back to Boston."

The words hang in the air like shattered glass. Sophie freezes, her hum cut short. My breath catches. The storm outside seems to pause, listening. Stuart looks up slowly from his plate. His smile comes, but it's tight and hard, pulled across his face like fabric stretched thin. His eyes are bright and cold.

"This is your home now," he says calmly. "Boston was never truly home. The lodge is where we all belong."

Amelia doesn't flinch. Her chin lifts a fraction, her dark eyes fierce.

"It doesn't feel like home. It feels..." She hesitates, then blurts, "It feels like a prison."

My chest constricts.

"Amelia," I whisper, trying to soothe and soften the word that cuts so sharp.

Stuart sets his knife and fork down with careful precision. He leans back in his chair, folding his hands, studying her as though she's a specimen on display.

"Ungrateful," he says finally.

The word is soft, but it carries weight. He doesn't raise his voice. He doesn't need to. Amelia's lips press together. Her fists clench in her lap. Sophie stares at her sister, wide-eyed, then ducks her head as though hiding will make her invisible. My instinct to protect her rises, hot and fierce. I reach across the table, touching Amelia's hand.

"She's adjusting," I say quickly. "It's new for all of us."

Stuart's eyes flick to me. His smile doesn't waver, but I see the warning there, sharp beneath the calm.

"She must learn gratitude," he says evenly. "This house offers her everything she needs. Warmth, shelter, family. What more could a child want?"

"A choice," Amelia whispers.

The silence that follows is unbearable. The storm batters the glass, the fire snaps and crackles, but in the room, there is nothing but the thrum of blood in my ears, and his cold, calculating silence. I squeeze Amelia's hand under the table, my own trembling. Her eyes meet mine, both pleading and defiant at once. Stuart lifts his glass, sipping as though nothing has happened. But his gaze lingers on Amelia, steady and unblinking, until she looks away.

When the meal ends, Sophie scurries from the room without a word. Amelia follows, her back straight, her head high. I want to go after them, to gather them both into my arms, to promise safety. But Stuart's hand closes over mine, anchoring me to my chair.

"She will learn," he says softly. "In time."

His smile returns, smooth and practiced. But in his eyes I see the same sharpness he used on me when he caught me with Isobel's jewelry box. The same warning, cold and absolute. His need for control is no longer aimed only at me. It has turned toward my children. And I will never forgive myself if I let him break them.

At bedtime, I move quietly down the hallway. The Blue Suite looms behind me, its velvet curtains choking out what little moonlight might creep in. I can't bear its perfume tonight. Not yet. My heart is heavy, and my thoughts are restless. I push open the girls' door.

Sophie is curled on the narrow bed, her small frame trembling beneath the quilt. The soft light from the bedside lamp glimmers on her damp cheeks, her lashes stuck together with tears. Amelia lies on the other bed, turned toward the wall, her back rigid, her fists knotted in the blanket. She is awake. I can tell by the way her shoulders rise and fall, sharp and deliberate, but she pretends otherwise, letting her silence speak for her.

"Mommy," Sophie whispers, sitting up when she sees me. Her voice cracks, small and raw. "I want my toys. I want my friends. I don't like it here."

My heart clenches. I cross to her quickly, gathering her into my arms. She buries her face against my chest, her little body wracked with quiet sobs.

"I know, sweetheart," I murmur, stroking her hair. "I know it's strange and scary. But it won't always feel this way. We'll make it ours. We'll find new games, new adventures. You'll see."

She shakes her head fiercely. "I don't want new. I want my old things. I want to go home."

Her words pierce me. Home. Boston. Our cramped little apartment, with crayons ground into the carpet and a stove that sometimes rattled when it heated. It was messy, precarious, exhausting. But it was ours, and it was a freedom I didn't recognize until it was taken from us.

Tears prick my own eyes, but I force them back.

"I promise," I whisper, kissing the crown of her head. "It'll get better. You'll feel safe here. You'll make new memories. And I'll be with you every step."

Her sobs quiet a little, her breathing evening out against my chest. I rock her gently, humming a lullaby I used to sing when she was a baby, about stars and safe journeys. For a moment, it almost feels like the world outside this room doesn't matter. Just me and my little girl, her trust like a fragile flame in the dark.

But then the floorboard behind me creaks, and I turn my head to see Stuart standing in the doorway. His arms are folded and his eyes are sharp, cold, piercing straight through me. I freeze, Sophie still in my arms. Amelia doesn't move, but I know she's listening, every muscle in her body taut. When he speaks, his voice is quiet, but it slices like a blade.

"She must learn."

My mouth goes dry. "She's frightened. She misses home."

He steps into the room, his boots silent on the rug.

"This is her home now. She must accept it. And you..." His gaze pins me, hard, absolute. "You mustn't encourage her weakness."

The words hit me like a slap. I clutch Sophie tighter, instinctively protective. My stomach knots so tightly I feel sick.

"She's a child," I whisper, my voice shaking despite myself. "Children cry. They need comfort."

His smile comes then, but it's thin and dangerous.

"Children need guidance. Comfort is fleeting. Discipline lasts."

Sophie whimpers against me, sensing the tension even if she doesn't understand the words. Amelia shifts under her blanket, finally turning her head just enough to glare at him, her small jaw set. My brave girl, always braver than she should have to be. I stroke Sophie's back, trying to calm her, but my heart hammers. Stuart takes another step closer.

"You'll spoil her," he says softly. "You'll trap her in weakness. Is that what you want?"

My throat tightens. "No."

"Then teach her strength."

The silence after his words is unbearable. Finally, he steps back, his smile smoothing into something almost gentle.

"You're tired," he says. "You don't see clearly. In time, you'll understand what real strength is."

He leaves as quietly as he came, the door closing behind him with a soft click. His footsteps fade down the hall. I sit frozen, with Sophie trembling in my arms, Amelia watching from her bed, her eyes fierce. I smooth Sophie's hair again, whispering reassurances I no longer believe. My hands tremble. Because I know, in that moment, with terrible clarity, if I don't find a way to protect them, I'll lose them.

10

The first time I leave the lodge, the air feels almost alien. Snow crunches underfoot, crisp and loud in the silence of the forest. My breath drifts out in pale ribbons, the cold sharp enough to sting my throat. The car Stuart arranged waits at the foot of the stone steps, its black paint dulled by frost. Mrs. Lennox is already inside, her posture as rigid as always.

Stuart kisses my cheek before I climb in. His lips linger, his hand pressing the curve of my hip.

"You'll be quick," he says, not a question. "There's nothing in town you need that we can't provide here."

I smile, obedient, and slide into the seat beside Mrs. Lennox. The driver pulls away, tires crunching through drifts, the trees blurring past in tall, dark walls. For a while, no one speaks. Mrs. Lennox stares straight ahead, her profile carved in stone. I watch the snow-shrouded landscape slip by. The world outside the lodge looks vast, endless, but also empty.

It takes nearly half an hour before the trees thin and the village appears, huddled in the valley like a clutch of survivors. Smoke curls from chimneys. The church steeple rises above the rooftops, its bell faintly glinting under a dusting of snow. The car stops outside the general store, which is a squat building with a broad front window fogged with warmth from inside. Mrs. Lennox steps out first, brisk and efficient, her boots crunching on the packed snow. I follow, inhaling the smell of smoke and wood that lingers in the air.

Inside, the heat is immediate, rolling off the cast-iron stove near the counter. The air smells of pine and coffee grounds. Shelves crowd with tins, flour sacks, jars of preserves. Two men in thick coats chat by the stove, their laughter low, their glances curious when Mrs. Lennox sweeps past them. I linger near the door, unmoored. For the first time since our wedding, I feel the stirrings of normalcy, of ordinary people murmuring normal conversations, boots stomping snow from their soles, the hum of life unconnected to Stuart, to the lodge, to me.

Mrs. Lennox moves methodically along the shelves, ticking items from a small list. She doesn't look at me. She doesn't tell me to stay close, but the implication hangs in the air like a leash. I drift toward a display of postcards by the window. Most are faded, showing the mountains in autumn, the lake glimmering in the sun. A few show the lodge itself, its stone face rising above the trees. I pick one up, tracing the image with my thumb. In the picture, the lodge looks magnificent, but softened somehow, smaller than it feels in person. Less suffocating.

"Pretty, isn't it?"

The voice startles me. I glance up. A woman stands beside me, perhaps in her late forties, bundled in a wool coat the color of slate. Her hair is streaked with silver, her eyes sharp, assessing. She smiles faintly, though her gaze is direct, unflinching.

"You're the new wife," she says quietly. Not a question.

Heat rises to my cheeks. I manage a polite smile. "Yes. Ellen."

She nods, her lips pursed as though weighing the name.

"Moira O'Donnell." She extends her gloved hand. Her grip is

firm, her eyes never leaving mine. "My husband's the sheriff here."

A chill prickles down my spine, though her tone is calm, friendly even. She leans closer, lowering her voice so the others by the stove can't hear.

"Don't let him shut you up in that house."

My breath stutters. I glance instinctively toward Mrs. Lennox. She is still by the shelves, comparing tins, with her back to us. Moira continues, her voice barely above a whisper.

"His mother... she wasn't as perfect as he tells it, but she didn't just die."

The words slam into me. My heart stumbles, my mouth going dry.

"What do you mean?" I whisper.

Moira's eyes flick past me, sharp with caution.

"Careful. He has ways of finding things out." She leans back slightly, her smile resuming, polite, practiced, but her eyes remain fierce. "The past lingers in that house. It won't help to ignore it."

I want to grab her hand, beg her to explain, but Mrs. Lennox is suddenly there, her presence looming. She places a jar into her basket with a decisive click, her gray eyes slicing through me.

"Ready?" she asks, her tone curt.

I swallow hard, forcing a smile at Moira. "Nice to meet you."

Moira's lips quirk, but her eyes hold mine, steady, as though she's trying to pass me something intangible, some strength or warning.

"You too," she says.

Mrs. Lennox's gaze lingers on me a beat longer before she turns toward the counter. I follow, my pulse racing, Moira's words echoing in my mind. She didn't just die. The phrase clings to me like smoke. By the time we step back into the snow, the village feels different. The chatter of the store, the warmth of the stove, the smell of pine, all of it fades behind me. My chest is tight, my thoughts sharp with questions I can't ask.

The car door shuts with a heavy thud, sealing me back into silence.

The Blue Suite smells stronger when I return, as though the perfume in the air has thickened in my absence. The curtains are drawn tight, the light low. I set my gloves on the dresser, my heart still racing with Moira's words. She didn't just die. The phrase replays, louder, heavier, until it fills the room. Her room.

I sit on the edge of the bed, pressing my hands together, trying to steady myself. But my mind keeps circling. What did Moira mean? What happened to Isobel? Why would Stuart hide it? The door opens and Stuart steps inside, closing it behind him with deliberate care. His eyes go straight to me, sharp and searching.

"You're quiet," he says, his voice smooth but edged. "You seem distracted."

I force a smile, though my lips tremble. "I'm just tired. The trip into town wore me out, I think."

His gaze narrows. He crosses the room, slow, deliberate, until he stands before me. His presence fills the space, the air shifting around him.

"Did anyone speak to you?" he asks softly.

The lie forms before I can stop it. "No. Only Mrs. Lennox. And the clerk at the store."

His eyes bore into mine, unblinking. The silence stretches between us. Then he cups my face in his hands, his grip tender but unyielding, his thumbs brushing my cheeks as though I'm fragile glass.

"No one out there understands us," he says, his voice low, steady, and almost hypnotic. "Only I do. Remember that."

His grip tightens, not painfully, but firmly enough that I cannot look away. His eyes gleam, dark and possessive, and I feel both cherished and trapped in the same breath.

"I know," I whisper, though my voice cracks.

He kisses me then, slow but demanding, his mouth claiming mine, sealing the lie inside me. His devotion presses close, smothering me. When he pulls back, his smile is tender again.

"Good girl. Rest now. You'll feel better."

He leaves the room, closing the door softly behind him. I sit frozen on the bed, my skin tingling where his hands held me. My heart pounds, not with relief but with terror. For the first time, I have lied to him. I've chosen silence over obedience. And though the lie might have saved me tonight, I know one day he'll see it in my eyes. The first crack has formed in my armor, and if he finds it, everything will shatter.

11

The snow continues through the night. I know because I've been lying awake, watching it flurry past the window and seeing the curtains swaying gently as if the wind is trying to force its way in. The timbers of the lodge creak and moan, their voices deep and tired, as though they've weathered one too many winters and might finally give in.

Stuart sleeps beside me, his breath steady, heavy. Even in sleep, his body sprawls with ownership, his arm draped across me like a gate. I lie stiff beneath the weight of it, staring into the dark. I try to breathe evenly, to calm the restlessness crawling under my skin. But the perfume of the Blue Suite is thick tonight. Isobel's presence seems stronger when the storm rages, as though the house itself exhales her into the air.

I ease from under his arm, careful not to wake him. The floorboards bite cold against my bare feet. The fire has died down, only embers glowing faintly in the grate. The shadows twitch across the walls like restless figures. I tell myself I only want to walk, to stretch, to bleed off this nervous energy. But my eyes keep drifting to the dresser, with the gowns folded neatly, the perfumes that stain the air. And beyond them, the forbidden box that I haven't touched since. And what else?

A gust of wind rattles the window harder. Stuart stirs, turning onto his side. I wait, holding my breath, until his breathing evens again. Then I cross the room, feeling my hands trembling. I open the bottom drawer, the stiff wood sticking slightly before sliding out. Beneath the silk gowns, I find a gap. Just enough space where fabric doesn't sit flush with the wood. My fingers probe, brush against something solid. Another box.

It's smaller than the jewelry case, covered in dust, as if it hasn't been opened in years. I pull it free, my pulse racing. The latch sticks, but with a sharp tug, it snaps open.

Inside I find a thin, leather-bound book, the pages filled with words. It's a diary, by the look of it. The handwriting inside is neat at first, delicate and precise. Words unfurl across the page like lace.

'January 12. The snow is heavier this year. The lodge feels colder, though the fires burn all day. He says the cold keeps us honest, that it purges weakness. I try to believe him.'

I flip further.

'February 3. I feel myself fading. He watches me constantly. He says perfection is the least I owe him. I polish the silver until my hands blister. I smile until my face aches. Still, he finds me lacking.'

A shiver runs through me.

'February 28. I dream of escape, but the forest presses close. There is no path but the one he chooses. I wonder sometimes if the lodge is not a house at all but a tomb, and I am only another relic inside it.'

I swallow down a feeling of nausea. The words echo in my thoughts. Fading. Lacking. Trapped. Those words could be mine. I flip further, pages trembling beneath my fingers. The handwriting grows frantic, loops less steady, ink blotched.

'March 14. He told me again. I must be stronger. I must endure. But I am tired. I am not what he wants me to be. Perhaps no one ever could be.'

The diary feels alive in my hands, the voice of another woman whispering across decades, telling me she once felt what I feel now. That she was pressed, molded, diminished. That she longed for escape.

My throat aches. I clutch the book against me as if it were a lifeline. I hear the bed creak behind me, and I freeze. He's awake. I whip around to see him sitting up, his face carved with fury, hard and unyielding. His eyes drop immediately to the diary clutched in my hands. For a heartbeat, the storm outside seems to still.

"What," he says softly, dangerously, "are you doing?"

The diary trembles in my grip. "I couldn't sleep. I was just..."

He swings his legs out of bed, stands with slow determination, and walks over to me. His steps are slow, deliberate, and threatening. I find myself recoiling, and trying not to.

"You mustn't disturb her things." His voice is low, taut, vibrating with suppressed rage. "How many times must I tell you?"

I open my mouth, but no words come. My throat is dry, my tongue heavy.

He holds out his hand. "Give it to me."

Every instinct screams to obey. My fingers twitch, but I can't let go. Some stubborn spark in me clings to the diary as though it is the only proof that I am not losing my mind. Or that someone else, once, saw this house for what it was.

His eyes narrow. He steps closer, looming. "Ellen."

The sound of my name in that tone of voice breaks me. I extend the diary with shaking hands. He takes it slowly, reverently, as though handling something sacred. But, unlike the jewelry box, he doesn't set this aside. Instead, he flips it open, his eyes scanning the page. A tight, cruel smile curves his mouth.

"Read it."

My heart jolts. "What?"

"Read it aloud." He thrusts the book toward me. "If you're so curious, read her words. Let me hear them from your mouth."

"I... Stuart, please..."

"Now."

The word cracks like a whip. My hands tremble as I take the diary back. My eyes blur, but I force them to focus. The ink swims in the firelight. I read, my voice thin, breaking:

"He wants me to be perfect, but I am fading."

My chest aches with tension and fear, my breathing is so shallow I feel lightheaded. Stuart's gaze never leaves me. He drinks in every word, his expression dark, his eyes sharp and fevered.

"I dream of escape, but the forest presses close. There is no path but the one he chooses."

My voice falters. Tears sting my eyes. I glance up, hoping for mercy. But he only tilts his head, his smile colder.

"Continue."

The words scrape my throat. My hands shake so violently the pages rustle. "Perhaps no one ever could be what he wants. Perhaps perfection is death itself."

I choke on the last word, and the silence swells between us, thick and unbearable. I break. I drop the diary onto the quilt and cover my face with my hands, sobbing. The sound bursts out of me raw, jagged, uncontrollable. Weeks of exhaustion, fear, longing, it all pours out at once. Stuart watches me dispassionately. He doesn't move at first. Then, slowly, he sits beside me. His hand strokes my hair, and for a moment it feels almost tender.

"Fragile," he murmurs. "Just like her."

His voice softens, coaxing. "You see now, don't you? How weak she was. How easily she broke."

I flinch, pulling back, but his hands catch my face, holding me still. His eyes gleam with an intensity that chills me to the bone.

"You must be stronger," he whispers. "Stronger than she ever was. You will not fade. You will not fail me."

His thumb strokes my cheek, wiping away tears, though his grip is iron. His smile is gentle, almost loving. But it cuts deeper than rage ever could. He doesn't want a wife, he wants a monument. A living testament to his control, stronger where she was weak, compliant where she resisted. And I, trembling under his hands, realize I am already becoming exactly that.

12

The Blue Suite feels even more stifling than it has before. I lie still, pretending to sleep, eyes closed to keep myself in the dark just a little longer. Stuart is awake. I know it in the way his breathing isn't quite even, the way his arm, draped over me, is a weight rather than a comfort, like a quiet reminder of ownership. When I shift, he lifts his head without speaking. We are two people pretending we are not watching each other.

"I can't breathe in here," I whisper finally. It's the smallest act of honesty I allow myself anymore.

He is up so quickly it feels like he's been waiting for the moment.

"Then we'll get you air," he says. Not a question or a suggestion, but a cold instruction. He reaches for my wrist. His fingers are cool. "Come."

"I need my gown," I murmur, but he is already moving, and I am already following, because the fastest way through a command is sometimes to obey it.

The corridor is ribbed with shadow, lights turned down so low they barely warm the darkness. The cold sharpens the deeper into the house we go, down the back staircase, past the wide hall with the portraits that look like they are choosing a side. At the mudroom, he lifts a heavy coat from a peg and drapes it over my shoulders without any tenderness. Mrs. Lennox is nowhere to be seen. I don't call out for her. I don't think she would come anyway.

He unlatches the iron bolts on the service door himself. The wind shoulders through the crack like a furious animal. He smiles into it, teeth white in the dark.

"Reflection requires some real weather," he says, almost kindly. "You'll understand soon. We all need a night to listen to the snow."

A night. The phrase lands like a wet garment on my skin.

"Stuart..." I start, but cold and fear steal the rest. He guides me across the back steps, down into the churned yard where drifts have formed small white walls. The snow lifts sideways, needling my cheeks and eyes. The world is sound and cold and the smell of pine. Somewhere to our left is the lake. I can feel its flatness, like a blank sheet in the black. Ahead, is the small, hunched square of deeper dark under the trees that I know is the cabin.

I've seen it by daylight, with its bare boards, a low roof that sags in the middle, and a single window like a blind eye. The girls had called it a "tiny house" and begged to explore. I said someday. It's strange how often someday is a synonym for never.

He pulls the door and it scrapes open, then sticks on snow. He pulls harder, and it gives with a little sigh. Inside is shadow stacked on shadow. The air has a wet, iron smell, as if water has been freezing and thawing in the grain of the wood for a hundred years.

"There," he says, voice bright with the satisfaction of a solution. "You said you needed air."

I step inside. The cold here is animate, a thing with hands that explore the seams of your clothing. There is a cot in the corner, a bucket, a peg with a coil of old rope. No stove. No rugs. The single window is dirty and smeared.

"Take a blanket." He tosses one from the cot as if revealing a party trick. It's thin, army-green, the kind of wool that promises itch, not heat.

"This is..." I begin, and fail to finish. Cruel? Punishment? The wrong word will make me defenseless.

"Reflection," he repeats, softer now. He steps close, the wind bulging the door against his back, his face a pale oval in the dark.

"You touch what must not be touched, you wander where you should not wander, your head fills with the grime of town. You won't listen to me in the warmth. So listen to the cold." He touches two fingers to my forehead as if in benediction. "You'll leave here clear."

"For how long?"

"Until you hear it," he says. "By morning, at the earliest." He kisses my forehead, an almost fatherly touch that curdles in my gut. "Don't be afraid. The forest belongs to us."

Then he is out, and the door comes to with a flat thud. The iron latch drops from the outside with a finality that feels like a verdict. I stand there holding the blanket, the darkness around me thinning only where a seam of moonlight slips at the window's edge. My breath puffs into the cold and hangs there, visible, as though my despair has been given shape. The wind needles through the gaps in the logs, finding my wrists, ankles, the tender hollow below my ears. When I sit on the cot, the canvas groans in a low, disappointed voice.

I wrap the blanket around my shoulders and it does what it can, which is to say, almost nothing. I pull up my coat's collar and tuck my hands into the sleeves. The first shiver is theatrical, my body's way of asking Are we truly doing this? The second is less polite.

"You'll leave here clear," I mimic in a bitter whisper, because if I don't say something in my own voice I will vanish entirely.

The wind labors for a while, then reshapes itself into a steady throw of snow. Sound is a geography of its own here. The trees creak and ease, creak and ease. The lake's frozen surface ticks and squeals as the ice shifts. I try to think of warm things. Of the girls asleep with their breaths out of sync, two little steam engines. Of soup thick with barley. Of Rachel laughing so hard she had to sit on the floor. But the body obeys the room it's in. The cold moves inward. Feet first, then calves. After a while, I can't tell if my teeth are chattering or if the whole cabin is.

Even the minutes are thicker here. Without a clock, time inverts. You can feel every second's weight and yet you're certain entire hours have disappeared. I lay down on the cot to fool my body into rest. The canvas is as unforgiving as a rebuke.

The first howl begins like a question thrown into the dark night. I sit up so fast the cold takes a bite out of my lungs. I listen keenly, waiting. Another howl, closer. That eerie vowel that's not music and not speech, something from a place older than both. A second voice answers it across the lake, sounding thinner, but more urgent. Then more, a ladder of sound. Wolves. I picture them without meaning to. They're dark shapes shifting at the tree line, noses lifted, breath pluming into the same air I share. The cabin is nothing to them but a line of boards, a wooden box full of human smell.

Reason speaks first. The door is stout, the wolves want deer, not people. Fear clears its throat afterward and reminds me that they want whatever they can get.

I slide off the cot and drag it with me, inch by inch, until its short legs catch on the floor. I lean my shoulder into it. The old rope on the peg becomes a lifesaver. I loop it clumsily around the cot frame and then the door handle. It's theater, probably, but theater is one way to pray.

Another howl, right outside the wall, low enough that I can feel it through the boards. A paw scrapes, or a twig, or my imagination, but the sound peels the top layer off my composure anyway. I press my spine to the door. The cold there is a knife that slides up under my coat like a patient hand.

"Go away," I whisper, and hate the pleading sound of it.

The rope stays taut. The door holds. I match my breathing to the wind until the howls move on, stitched back into the larger noise of the night. When my muscles stop locking, I realize I'm shaking in a constant juddering rhythm that I simply can't control. Cold and fear control me now.

The mind opens peculiar drawers when it's freezing. It hoards small oddities, like little trinkets of thought. In the tight, air-bitten dark of the cabin, something I have kept sealed for years slips its latch. Michael. I haven't said his name aloud in so long I'm not sure it would come out right. Michael Dalton. He is a silhouette at first, a tall laugh, a firefighter's jacket thrown over the back of a chair, the stink of smoke and sweat and happiness that takes a whole shower to shift. He was always warm in winter, always running toward what others fled. "Brave," people said in the way they say "reckless" when there are casseroles on the table.

We met over paper cups of weak coffee at a charity pancake breakfast where he burned his hand without flinching and I realized I was doomed to love him. He had a way of looking at the world like it was a dare. He also forgot rent, and took double shifts, and came home with his eyelashes singed and stories he told only to the ceiling because he didn't want to make me afraid. "I'm fine," he'd say, blowing on a blister like he could cool the danger with air. "It's what I'm for."

When Amelia was born, he was terrified of how small she was, and then he cried when she gripped his finger with her whole hand. Sophie came five years later, after a season of overtime and a promise to slow down that lasted three weeks. He loved them with a ferocity that was sometimes a friend and sometimes a fire in the room.

The night he died, the city had cold so fierce the gutters cracked. A triple-decker off Dorchester went up with the kind of speed you only see when the air itself wants fuel. He ran inside with his partner and the roof went. So did the stairs. Everyone in the neighborhood stood outside with steam coming off their mouths like prayers. When they hauled him out, he was still wearing his pilot's grin, like the afterimage of a man who thought he could beat it this time too.

After the funeral, casseroles swarmed my kitchen like a terrible flock. Bills mounted. Overtime dries up when the person who worked it is in the ground. There were benefits, sure, and promises. There are always promises. The debts came like a slow leak, starting small, but ceaselessly ebbing, impossible to find the hole. I slept in hour-long pieces. The world felt tilted. There is nothing to be done but live anyway.

Thomas arrived later, a different kind of man. Drier. A man who would never run into a burning building because he would never be near one. He adopted the girls because he loved me, he said, and because it made everything tidy for the courts. He loved me like a contract, like a schedule. And things went along until they didn't. His absence was quieter than death and, in some ways, meaner. But the girls called him "Daddy" because he was the daily man, the one who made lunches when I worked late, the one who drove carpool until he didn't. Sophie has only known him. She was too young when Michael died to ever know him as her real Daddy. In all the ways that matter to a school form, Thomas is their father. In all the ways that matter to my bones, Michael is the first story I tried to delete.

What did I want when I said yes to Stuart? Not romance. Not really. Not the heat of Michael, not the thin steadiness of

Thomas. I wanted a door that closed and stayed closed. I wanted a bill that paid itself. I wanted someone else to hold the heavy end for once. Security is a soft word until it becomes the pillow over your face.

I press harder against the cabin door. The cold walks up my spine like fingers.

"I'm sorry," I say to the dark, and I'm not sure whether I'm apologizing to Michael for moving on, to the girls for bringing them here, or to myself for the gall of wanting rest.

Somewhere near dawn, the wind changes its voice again from fury to fatigue. The cabin seems to sweat a little, a dampness at the seams. I stop shivering in the showy way and start to tremble deep, an engine too slow to do any good. The blanket has become little more than a suggestion. I pull my legs toward my chest. Pins and needles arrive like wasps, then depart. There's a slipping feeling at the edges of experience, like falling asleep at the wheel.

A sound drags me back. Footsteps. Not the delicate embroidery of curious paws, but heavy boots. The crunch changes near the threshold where the snow thins. The latch lifts. The rope goes taut. I gasp and sit up straighter, my shoulder welded to the door, my weight ridiculous against the iron and wood that would happily decide without me.

The latch rattles again. "Ellen," Stuart's voice says, surprisingly soft, like I am a thing he has misplaced and discovered again. "Open this door."

I untie the rope with clumsy, biteless fingers. The knot has half frozen to itself, and my nails do nothing to loosen it. He stays patient, then less so, then something brittle creeps into his tone. "Open it now."

It takes both hands and my teeth, and when it gives, the rope slaps my knuckles and they sing. The door drops outward a fraction. Cold light sifts in around him from a winter dawn that looks like the sun has given up being warm and is trying a different approach. He fills the doorway the way men like him fill rooms. He looks at me as if I have proved something for him.

"Well?"

My mouth makes a sound before my brain picks a word. "Cold."

His smile is microscopic. "Yes."

I step past him into the morning because anything is better than the cabin, even if that anything is him. The lake is a plate of pewter. The trees hold their snow like winter coats. The lodge is a black geometry against the pale. For a half second, the house looks new to me, as if last night's storm has washed off its disguise and left the structure, naked and unapologetic. A machine built to trap weather and women.

"Reflection," he says again, as if we are in a class and I am the only student who didn't study for the test. "What did you hear?"

I swallow. Dry sounds dangerous. "Wolves."

Another one of those almost-smiles. "And in yourself?"

I want to say fear, and loss, and betrayal. And spite. The thin wire that stays when you burn everything else.

"Clarity," I say instead, because it's true and also gives him what he wants.

He nods once, satisfied.

"Good."

He takes my elbow. His grip is not cruel, but it assumes. It assumes my direction, my pace, my consent. We cross the snow-dumb yard. At the steps, he pauses as if remembering a line he was meant to deliver. He leans in and kisses my temple in a way a stranger would read as tenderness.

"You see," he says into my hair. "The world can't touch you here. Only I can."

I think of Michael's hands, raw and hot, holding me at the

stove so he could dance me around until we burned the rice together and laughed when we ate it anyway. I think of Thomas folding a damp dish towel perfectly in half and then in half again because that's what he knew how to fix. I think of both of them and see how I arrived at this door. The ache that comes is complicated and immediate.

Inside the mudroom, he sheds my coat like a skin and hangs it precisely on the peg. He does not ask if I am warm. The house closes around us the way the lake ice thickens, incrementally, inexorably, a soundless work.

In the Blue Suite later, when the girls sneak in at noon with pink noses and Sophie's hair damp at the ends from snow and Amelia's chin set at the particular angle it gets when she has decided to save me from something she cannot name, I make hot chocolate in a jug I shouldn't use without asking and we sit on the floor with our backs to the bed and our legs stretched toward the grate. I do not tell them where I was. I do not tell them about the wolves. I tell them a story about a fox that found a cabin and made it a house until the storm was tired and then went back to being an outdoor fox again.

"Is the fox you?" Sophie asks, deadpan, because five-year-olds are mediums.

"Maybe," I say.

Amelia watches me over the rim of her mug, and I can see in her eyes that she already knows about the rope on the door without ever having seen it.

When they return to their room under the pretense of building a fortress with quilts, I stand at the window with my palm on the cold glass and decide a thing I will not write down even in my head. I am done mistaking security for safety. I am done confusing silence with love.

Stuart passes the doorway just then, two fingers trailing the frame, all ownership, as if he painted the house into existence and it shaped itself accordingly. He pauses, smiles, and keeps going. He believes last night cured me of questions. Let him. The wolves will be back, of course. That's what hunger does. It circles and waits. It tests the door again. The difference now is small and private, but enormous in another way. The next time something howls, I will not be the thing holding the door closed from inside. I will be the hand on the latch.

13

The study always feels like the only warm room in the lodge, but tonight the fire is even more alive. It's popping and snapping, throwing copper flares, driving shadows up the bookshelves in nervous climbs. The room smells of smoke and old bindings and a trace of turpentine from the canvases he keeps leaning along the walls like sleeping sentries. Portraits watch from their frames with the familiar Drummond jaw, every gaze a verdict. Outside, the wind scours the shutters, and a branch taps at the glass like a persistent thought.

Stuart sits in the armchair by the hearth with his drink untouched, shoulders squared as always, but something in him has lost its armor. For once, he isn't wearing the smile that organizes a room. His hands are bare of gestures. He's looking into the fire as though a face he knows might form there.

"I should tell you," he says at last, and the words hang like a fragile bridge between us. "No one ever asks the right questions, so it is simpler not to answer. But you... you ask without even meaning to."

I'm perched on the edge of the other chair, my legs tucked

under me for warmth. The Blue Suite still clings to my clothes, that powder-sweet scent I can't wash out. My pulse ticks a little fast. Vulnerability here is a shifting thing. It's an invitation one moment, trap the next. Still, I nod.

"Then tell me."

He breathes once, as if preparing to lower himself beneath cold water.

"She was the heart of this place," he says softly. "My mother. Luminous. The house obeyed her. If she laughed, the doors unlatched and the drafts quieted. If she cried..." He swallows. "It stormed even when the sky was clear."

In the firelight, his face looks younger and also more gaunt, like a mask has slipped and left the bone map beneath. He glances at the piano against the far wall. It is always closed, a dark mouth without teeth.

"She played every evening. Chopin, sometimes Debussy when she dared. You could tell how the day had gone by which key she struck first."

He doesn't look at me when he speaks. His eyes are fixed somewhere beyond the flames, a room behind the room. A little boy under the piano. The picture unfolds itself in my head as he speaks, as if he's handed it to me and I am developing it under the red light of the fire. Small hands flat on the rug, the underside of the instrument a black cathedral of wood and strings. Mother's foot working the pedal, slipper heel scuffed, blue silk hem brushing the top of his ears. Music hanging above him like weather.

"My father..." The word leaves his mouth like iron scraped across stone. "He liked order."

He smooths invisible dust from the arm of the chair.

"He believed obedience was not a virtue but a fact. Like gravity. Or winter." His mouth curves, but it isn't a smile. "He would stand in doorways and watch. To be watched by him was to have your skin pulled tight."

I think of the diaries, the ink that turned frantic in Isobel's hand. He wants me to be perfect, but I am fading. The fire pops. Stuart flinches, then stills as if ashamed of the flinch.

"She was frail," he continues, his voice softening into that private reverence reserved for the dead. "Delicate, he used to say, like he was praising a vase. Nerves, they called it then. But to me she was..." He searches the air with his fingers as though feeling for a word. "...light. She was what the house kept trying to speak."

The boy crawls forward until his cheek presses to his mother's ankle. She doesn't look down because not-looking is safety, but she shifts her foot just enough to touch him with the side of her shoe. A secret language. Her hands flutter briefly from the keys, hover, return. In the doorway, a tall shape with a glass in his hand clears his throat. The melody tenses as if it knows it is being judged.

"She protected me," Stuart says, now watching his own hands as if they might betray him. "From him. From the rules. From the lodge, even. She made small worlds inside big rooms. Our twilights were filled with blankets and stories in wardrobes. She would say, 'You are only mine, aren't you?' and I would say, 'Yes,' and mean it."

He looks up with a sudden nakedness I didn't expect.

"I was hers, and only hers."

The sentence hangs in the warm air, cooling as it settles. It is a confession and a boast and a wound.

"She made me her task," he adds, quieter. "Her purpose. And I..." He moves his shoulders like a man adjusting a weight that was put there long ago. "I was good at being saved."

The fire hisses. I feel the study leaning around us, listening. The portraits do not blink.

"What about him?" I ask. I keep my voice even. When I imagine his father, I imagine a vertical line through coat, belt, and expectations.

He says the next words like pulling splinters one by one.

"He believed love softens the spine. He would come into the music room with his hands in his pockets and walk around the piano as if inspecting a beast he had bought. He would list what he'd paid for. The tuition, repairs, wood for the winter, the new roof on the west wing. And she would keep playing, but softer and softer, like a woman backing down a corridor from a man who will not stop advancing."

In my mind's eye, the boy doesn't breathe. He knows the sound of his father's voice, like wool pulled tight over sharp things. He knows the smell of him. A cold wool coat and winter air and the sourness on his breath that meant this glass is not the first. The mother's right hand misses a note. The father says her name as if it is a small offense. She begins again from the top.

"I heard what children aren't meant to hear," Stuart says, and his voice has the practiced blankness of someone stepping onto thin ice. "Not once. Not sometimes. Always. Doors don't hold back sound in this house. They funnel it. They aim it right at your heart."

He takes up his glass, doesn't drink. The liquid smokes the crystal like captured fire.

"They would fight in the study after guests left. My father would close the curtains even at night. He said light breeds gossip."

"What about your mother?"

"She cried where no one could see. In the Blue Suite. You can still smell her fear in there." His glance finds me, swift, clinical. "You've smelled it."

I don't deny it. The diary's phantom weight sits in my lap, laced with perfume and panic.

"She would press her wrist to her mouth so the sounds would go back down," he says, and there is a faint astonishment in his tone, as though wondering how a body learns to do that?

"When he raised his voice, she would raise her music. When he raised his hand..." He doesn't finish it. He looks into the fire until I understand he won't finish it.

The boy in the flashback brackets his ears with his palms. The piano is an ocean above him, each chord a wave that breaks and retreats. A crack like a book slammed shut, a glass shattering its fragments. A woman saying "please" like a habit that used to work. Then a softer sound of persistent weeping, the rhythm of it finding the boy's heart and tugging it into sync. He crawls out and pads down the hall, bare feet cold on wood. He stops at the crack of the Blue Suite door and sees an ankle. It shakes as if the leg is carved from winter itself. He hears her say it, almost the way actors say lines on a stage they hate.

"If you leave me, I'll die."

Stuart speaks the sentence with a perfect memory of cadence and pitch. The fire seems to quiet for it.

"She meant it," he adds, but his mouth twists a little, as if even now he isn't sure. "Or she meant for him to believe it. I believed it. I was... very good at believing her. I would crawl into her wardrobe and push my face into her dresses because they smelled like violets and not like him, and I would promise to be perfect and strong and quiet. She would put her hand into the dark and find mine and say, 'My brave boy.'"

He laughs then, not kindly. "Bravery is easy when you are praised for it in closets."

Something in me loosens. A recognition of his pain, maybe, or dread of him repeating the cycle now. The shape of his childhood pushes itself against me until it fits.

"You loved her like a job," I say before I can edit myself. "And she loved you like a cure."

He doesn't flinch. He only tips his head, considering the truth of it as if it's a painting hung a little crooked.

"What else was there?" he asks simply. "He demanded obedience. She demanded adoration. The house demanded... continuity." He gestures to the portraits. "I learned to give everyone what they asked for and to keep the rest for her."

"The rest?"

"Myself." He finally drinks, and the swallow seems to cut on the way down. "I hid the parts of me that made him angry in the places that made her happy. I learned to hold my breath when I walked past his door. I learned to listen with my eyes. To the curve of her mouth after a guest said something unkind, to the tremor in the way she placed a teacup back in its saucer when she was holding in rage."

His glance flicks toward me, quick as a blade.

"And I learned to watch for the moment someone decides they will leave."

The room tilts a fraction. I think of the way his attention fixed on me in the Athenaeum as if fastening a brooch through skin. I think of how he says mine as if it heals him to hear it.

"What happened to her?" I ask, though I've read the shape of it in ink.

"She left in the only way that wouldn't betray her own rules," he says flatly. "She dissolved. It was a long, careful work. She missed meals and called it devotion. She forgot names and called it transcendence. She slept in the day and learned nocturnes at night as if darkness was the only place she could move without consequence. One October she began coughing. By February, she was speaking about me in the past tense."

He turns the glass in his fingers. Firelight fractures in it.

"He called doctors, she called priests. The doctors said rest, the priests said prayer. She said perfection and then stopped saying anything at all."

His face closes then, not with anger but with pride curdled into resentment.

"Weakness," he murmurs, almost to himself. "She let him define the terms. She taught me everything about love except how not to drown along with the person who can't swim."

We sit in the sound of the fire eating its way through a log. The smell of resin grows sweeter as the wood breaks.

"You loved her," I say softly, because the room needs a plain sentence to stand on.

"I was her purpose," he corrects, and the words are stripped to bone. "It isn't the same."

He leans back, closes his eyes, opens them again.

"When she died, the house turned on its axis. He moved through it like a man going through the motions. He told me I would step into the role that kept the place breathing. He called it legacy. I called it air I couldn't swallow." A small smile that has nothing to do with humor visits his mouth and leaves. "So I left. To school. To studios. To cities that did not care about my name. I thought distance could cauterize that awful inheritance."

"And did it?"

He considers. "It made it smaller, the way things get when you are far away. But smaller is not gone. The lodge kept a long finger on my collar. And when it tugged, I came back."

For yourself, I don't say. For the shrine, for the portrait, for the woman whose perfume is still arguing with the dust. For me, who arrived ready to be taught how to replace her. He sets his glass aside and looks at me fully for the first time since he began his story. The gaze is not the punishing one, not the proprietary one. It is the gaze of that boy under the piano, all pupils, all plea.

"You understand now," he says quietly. "Why I make rules.

Why I insist. She fell because no one held her upright. Because no one told her how to be strong."

Images flicker through my mind. My spine straightened by his fingers, the door of the cabin latch dropping from the outside, Sophie's tears, Amelia's chin set like a blade. My body remembers being cold down to the marrow and still, some traitorous part of me wants to take his face in my hands and say the sentence Isobel taught him: If you leave me, I'll die. Only I would mean if I leave this version of you, the one who believes love is a leash.

"I see what she asked of you," I say instead. "And what he demanded." I keep my voice steady. "And I see what you've asked of me."

His expression warms, misreading assent where there is analysis. "To be strong," he says. "To be better than her. To be the heart that does not fail."

The words land like coins dropped into a well. They keep falling.

"I think," I say carefully. "That she loved you so much she made you responsible for whether she lived. And that wasn't love. That was need."

He flinches as if I've touched a bruise. The old hardness rises like a reflex and a defense.

"She gave me everything."

"She gave you a burden no child should carry." My voice is almost a whisper. The wind presses at the shutters like someone listening at a door. "And you've been looking for someone to help you carry it ever since."

Silence opens. The fire pops. He studies me, the vulnerability sliding as the hard surface re-forms. I can see the choice in him. To open or close, admit or command. For a heartbeat, the boy wins. His mouth trembles and his eyes shine.

"If you leave me..." he begins, and then stops, startled by his own mouth choosing her sentence.

He laughs once, thin and sharp, and looks toward the piano instead. When he speaks again, the man has returned, all smooth, collected, and persuasive.

"You won't leave me," he says, and it's not a question. The firelight coins his certainty. "You understand me too well."

I grip my hands in my lap so he won't see them shake. Understanding is not the same as safety. Empathy is certainly not the same as love. I keep my eyes on the flames because if I meet his, he will make of my gaze a vow.

"I hear you," I say.

He relaxes as if that counts. While the wind charts the windows and the portraits keep watch, I tuck away what matters. The knowledge that Isobel loved him so tightly she thinned him out and then poured him into a mold shaped like herself. That his father hammered the mold and called it a home. And that I have been asked to set like plaster around both.

He leans forward and takes my hand, admiration and possession braided in his grip.

"You are luminous," he says, echoing his first word for her. The study approves with a gust in the chimney.

"You are strong," he adds, as if saying it makes it so.

In the fire's heat, I feel the chill of the cabin creep back into my bones, reminding me that strength and obedience are not twins. Love and enclosure are not two sides of the same coin. A boy under a piano learned the wrong lesson and grew into a man building the same room over and over, dragging his chosen into it and calling the closed latch a promise.

"I am," I say, and let the sentence end where he wants it, while inside I finish the thought he can't hear. I will not be yours in the way she was.

We sit in silence for a long while. There is little more to say.

His voice, when it comes, is quieter than before. But it carries a fevered edge.

"You think you're the first?"

I sit stiffly in the armchair, my hands pressed to the armrests as though they might anchor me.

"The first what?"

"The first woman I brought here. To the lodge." He stops pacing, turning toward me. The firelight glances off his cheekbones, sharpening his face into something dangerous.

"There were others. After she died. I thought I could find someone worthy. Someone who might understand."

A cold thread winds down my spine. "Worthy?" I echo, buying time.

He steps closer, his shadow swallowing the rug between us.

"They wanted my name. My money. The paintings, the inheritance. Trinkets." His mouth twists. "Not one of them cared for what mattered. Not one of them understood the devotion required."

The word devotion lands heavily, weighted with a meaning he hasn't defined but I already know. The same word Isobel used, perhaps, when she pressed her wrist to her lips and whispered she would die if he left her. I force my voice steady.

"And what happened to them?"

His eyes flick toward the fire, away from me, as though the answer smolders there.

"They betrayed me."

The silence stretches. I don't dare press further. Betrayal here could mean anything. It could mean leaving, refusing, or disappointing. All equal crimes in his eyes. He resumes pacing, his hands flexing at his sides.

"They weren't strong enough. They complained of the cold. The rules. They thought the lodge was a prison. Or a mausoleum. They didn't see it for the sanctuary it is." He turns on his heel sharply, facing me again. "They couldn't measure up to her purity."

Her. Isobel. Always the axis around which his life spins. The Blue Suite is not just a shrine, it is a test he has forced on every woman after her. My stomach knots. I see it so clearly now. He does not love me as myself. He never has. He loves me as an echo, a vessel, another attempt at resurrection.

He stops pacing altogether and strides toward me. His boots are soft on the rug, but the intent in each step is loud enough to shake me. He grips my wrists suddenly, his fingers iron around bone. The pain is sharp, immediate. I gasp, instinctively pulling back, but he holds fast. His eyes bore into mine, blazing with a desperate brightness.

"But you," he says, his voice low, trembling with urgency. "You are different."

My heart slams against my ribs. "Stuart..."

"You will never abandon me." His grip tightens until I wince. His face hovers close, the firelight catching in his pupils, making them look endless. "Promise me."

Terror coils in my throat. The room tilts. In that moment, I see what he needs from me. It's not partnership, not even love. It's a vow. The oath that binds me not just to him, but to his past, to his mother, to the house itself. I whisper because I have no choice.

"I won't abandon you."

His eyes close, and relief floods his face like a blessing. He releases me slowly, his thumbs gently brushing the red marks blooming on my wrists. Then he kneels, his forehead pressing briefly against the back of my hand, a gesture both worshipful and suffocating. When he looks up again, his smile is soft and boyish. Almost.

"Good girl."

The words pierce me. I sit frozen, the ache in my wrists

throbbing, the portraits above us staring with their cold, painted eyes. Inside, I understand the horror in full. I am not Ellen any more, not mother of Amelia and Sophie, not a woman with a past and her own wounds and her own choices. I am a vessel for his grief and his delusions. A mirror. A second chance to perfect the bond that consumed him and Isobel. And if I falter, if I betray him in any way, I know exactly what will happen. I will join the others who "didn't measure up."

14

The lodge has its own version of silence. It isn't emptiness, but layers of absent movement. Floorboards that sigh even when no one is walking on them, pipes stuttering low in the walls, the distant tick of radiators straining against the cold. Every sound feels amplified because the rest is so hushed. At night, it's unbearable.

I pad down the upstairs hallway. The portraits lining the walls tilt their gazes downward, endless generations of Drummonds watching me pass. The girls' door is open a crack. Inside, Sophie is asleep, sprawled diagonally across her quilt, her thumb pressed stubbornly into her mouth. Amelia sits on the floor by the bed, knees drawn up, her hair loose around her shoulders. She looks up when I step in, her eyes wide and alert.

"Mom," she whispers quickly, before I can even close the door. "I need to tell you something."

My stomach knots. I lower myself onto the floor beside her. The glow from the nightlight flickers across her serious face.

"What is it, sweetheart?"

Her hands twist in her lap, fingers fidgeting with the hem of her nightgown. "I heard him. Talking to Mrs. Lennox."

My throat tightens. "When?"

"Earlier. In the hall by the study." Her voice is urgent, hushed. "He didn't know I was there."

I glance toward the door, instinctively checking. The corridor is still.

"What did you hear?"

Amelia leans closer, her words quick, tumbling over each other.

"He said children can be broken into obedience. He said sometimes it takes time, and sometimes... it takes force. But he said all children can be made to listen if you're patient enough."

Ice floods my chest. For a moment I can't breathe.

"He was talking about me and Sophie," Amelia whispers, her eyes filling. "Wasn't he?"

I reach for her, pulling her against me, my arms wrapping around her shaking shoulders.

"He doesn't get to break you," I say fiercely, though my voice trembles. "Not you, not Sophie. Not while I have breath in my body."

She pulls back just enough to look at me, her eyes dark and determined.

"Then we have to leave, Mom. We can't stay here."

Her certainty cuts me. I want to shield her from the truth, to soften it with reassurances. But she's right. She's so perceptive and aware of the world around her. I nod, tears stinging my eyes.

"I know."

Her chin lifts, resolve hardening her young face. "I've been thinking. There are delivery trucks, right? That bring food and things? If we wait by the kitchen door when one comes, maybe slip out when nobody's looking. We could hide in the truck all the way back to town. Or wave down a car on the road."

The speed of her plan makes my heart ache. She's a child, but she's strategizing like a soldier.

"It's too dangerous," I whisper. "The forest, the snow..."

"Staying is more dangerous," she interrupts firmly. Her small fists clench in her lap. "He looks at us like... like we're not people. Like we're something he has to fix."

I smooth her hair, brushing it back from her face.

"You're right," I admit softly. "We have to be careful. If he suspects..."

"I know." Her voice is sharp with urgency. "We can't let him know."

Sophie stirs on the bed, rolling onto her side, murmuring in her sleep. Amelia and I both freeze until she settles again. I take Amelia's hand, pressing it tightly between mine.

"We'll watch. We'll wait. When the chance comes, we'll take it. But until then, you have to be careful. Don't let him see your anger."

Her eyes narrow. "I can't pretend forever."

"I know." My voice cracks. "But for now, please try. For Sophie's sake."

Her eyes fill again, but she nods. "Okay."

I pull her into me, holding her as if I can fold her back into my arms like when she was small. She smells of soap and of childhood straining to remain itself under impossible weight. As I rock her, my mind spirals. The lodge always feels like it's listening, its beams bending inward, its walls eavesdropping so that it can report back to its master. But in this small pocket of flickering light, I find something I thought I'd lost. It's the last dregs of my resolve. Amelia is no longer just my daughter. She is my ally. And her fierce, unflinching loyalty might be the only thing keeping us alive.

By evening, the storm has returned, the lodge rattling under its weight. The dining room glows with firelight, the table heavy with food Mrs. Lennox has prepared. The smell of roasted meat mixes with smoke, saturating the air.

Sophie chatters half-heartedly about a storybook, her little voice a bright thread trying to sew the silence together. Amelia sits rigid, her back straight, her plate untouched. Her eyes flick to me across the table, steady, reminding me of our whispered pact. Stuart sits at the head of the table, his presence dominating the room. He lifts his glass, his eyes fixed on me, and begins to speak.

"Family," he says, his voice carrying the weight of proclamation. "Family is the only pure thing left in this world. The world beyond these walls is a rot of corruption, greed, and weakness. Here, we preserve what matters. Here, we are unsullied."

His gaze sweeps over the girls, but returns always to me, burning.

"We are chosen," he continues, his tone rising like a sermon. "Bound together by more than blood. By devotion and sacrifice. Purity demands surrender. Only when we give all of ourselves to one another are we whole."

Amelia's fork clatters against her plate. She doesn't speak, but the defiance in her glare is unmistakable. Stuart's eyes catch hers. His smile tightens, just slightly, enough to bare a hint of teeth. The silence stretches, electric, until Sophie shifts uncomfortably in her chair, her eyes wide. I reach for Amelia's hand under the table, squeezing hard, begging silently. Don't. Not now. She doesn't squeeze back. Her hand is stone. Stuart sets down his glass with deliberate calm.

"Children must learn their place in the order of things. Obedience is not punishment, it is salvation."

Mrs. Lennox, standing by the sideboard, doesn't look up. Her face is expressionless, her hands hanging limply at her sides. Dinner drags on under the weight of his words. Every mouthful tastes of ash. The fire's heat feels oppressive, pressing sweat onto the back of my neck. When it ends, Stuart dismisses the girls with a nod. Sophie scurries out quickly, relief flooding her little shoulders. Amelia follows, but not before casting one last, sharp look at him, her chin raised in open challenge.

He notices. The moment the door closes behind them, he turns to me. His smile is gone. His eyes glint like steel.

"Your eldest," he says softly. "Needs firm guidance."

My heart pounds. "She's only a child. She's frightened."

"Defiance must be corrected early." He leans back in his chair, his voice deceptively gentle. "If you cannot provide that correction, I will."

The words drop like stones into a well. I swallow hard, forcing calm.

"I'll speak to her."

His gaze lingers, testing and probing mine. Then he nods, satisfied, and stands up. His hand brushes the back of my chair as he passes, a touch that is both possessive and a warning. The fire cracks behind him, the portraits staring down from the walls cry their silent warning. I am not the only one in danger. Amelia's defiance has made her a target. And if I cannot find a way out soon, my daughter will be the one he breaks first.

15

The wind has a particular voice when it comes off the lake at midnight. It's a long, hoarse wail, as if something out there is trying to speak through a throat full of ice. It threads itself through the seams of the windows and into the silk drapes, making them breathe in slow, uneasy gulps. Tonight, the Blue Suite feels saturated with the weight of its history, and it squashes me. I fall asleep with my knees pulled to my chest and the covers up over my ears like a child. When I dream, it doesn't feel like dreaming.

She is there, pale and luminous the way frost is luminous in lantern light, standing at the foot of the bed in a pale lilac dress that has the color of a bruise diluted with milk. Her hair is pinned tightly, as if fingers have had to press and pinch to tame it into obedience, and the skin at her temples shines damp. She is younger than the portraits, older than the letters. Her mouth trembles, but when she opens it, no sound comes out, just the damp-shimmering inhale before weeping. Her hands are empty. The gesture they make is not a reach out, but rather the opposite, a withdrawing. As if every part of her that wants to touch someone has been taught not to.

"Isobel," I try to say, but the name gets stuck. It feels like the room does not allow it to come out.

She looks at my hands where they grip the quilt and flinches like the sight wounds her. Then she lifts one finger and presses it to her lips the way a person does when they are listening for a sound they cannot afford to miss. Her gaze flicks to the wardrobe. To the dresser. To my lap. I'm not holding anything. But the weight is there. My arms know it, my wrists bend to cradle an object I cannot see. And then, in that strange way dreams rearrange themselves without moving, I am holding the diary. Its leather is cold. The edges of its pages fur my palms with dust. It's open, but the handwriting is not the calm lace I first found. These loops are violent. The lines lean as if the letters themselves are trying to run.

Behind Isobel, or behind the dream of her, there is a second stage. A corridor of mirrors where I glimpse another door opening, a shadow moving, a taller shape stepping out of the dark and bringing cold with it. I can't make him out. He is an absence. Every time I try, the wind throws itself against the window and the glass bows with a soft moan and I wake.

I wake choking on perfume. The room is black. I don't move for a moment, testing reality, and counting my breaths until they stop stuttering. And then I feel the same weight again. The diary sits open across my thighs. For a few seconds I am certain I'm still dreaming. I remember standing up after the confrontation, after reading the entries aloud for Stuart with tears blurring the ink, and I remember him hiding the book back under the gowns in the bottom drawer beneath a folded shawl that smelled of violet and old sorrow. I remember the sound of the drawer closing like a mouth.

I know I didn't take it out. The perfume thickens, cloying in the air. It stings the back of my throat. I reach for the lamp switch and then stop. I don't want light. Light will make this more real. I lift the diary, the leather colder than my skin, and tilt it toward the crack in the curtain where dawn's fingers are just reaching in. The weak light blanches the page, but the words rise anyway, splayed and frantic. 'He watches even when I sleep. I can feel him looking like a hand pressing me flatter and flatter to the mattress, as if he intends to iron me out until I am smooth and uncreased and empty of everything but his wanting.'

Another line below it, written smaller, as though crouching:

'He says I am weak. He says I belong only to him. He says love means not remembering yourself.'

My hands begin to shake. The diary trembles, the pages rustling like wings.

I turn another leaf. The handwriting dips, snatches itself back. The entries become lists, then prayers, then single phrases that repeat as if repetition might make them true: 'If I am perfect, the house will be kind.' 'If I am perfect, he will stop looking at me like a door he wants to shut from the outside.' 'If I am perfect, I will not need air.'

There are days with no dates. There are dates with no words. Then I find one which says, 'I dreamed a door was locked and the key hung around my neck and I could not remember how to lift my hands.'

The wind whistles in the chimney. I glance toward the foot of the bed before I can stop myself. The air there wavers with heat from the buried radiators. There's no figure there now, only that drape-breathing and the thick, sugared stink of a perfume someone poured into the walls. I whisper into my collar, almost afraid to disturb the room.

"Did you die here?"

It's a terrible question. It makes me feel like a ghoul. But I also need to know where the end came. Whether these curtains trapped the last of her air. Whether this bed, these quilts, this mirror, were the last witnesses. There is no voice in answer. Only a tiny sound across the room, like a distinct, private click, like a bottle's glass stopper settling deeper into its throat. One of the perfumes on the dresser, perhaps? Heat shifting wood? Or the house answering me in its own way. I swallow and look down again. The ink on the last lines has bled into the fiber, as if tears fell there and the paper drank them, but I can still read it.

'If there is a mercy it is snow. It covers and covers. Even footprints. Even blood.'

My hands are cold where they touch the diary. It is just a book, I tell myself. Just paper and ink. Her story. Not mine.

"Isobel," I say again, and this time the name comes. Speaking it makes me feel disloyal, as if the room itself is an altar and I've said something profane. "What did he..." I can't finish the sentence. "What did they do to you?"

Thunderless lightning flares somewhere beyond the forest, and the window glows for a heartbeat with its flat, extraterrestrial light. In that white blink the suit of the room becomes a negative image. The framed mirror looks like a dark door, the quilt's lilies reverse to skeletal ribs. The diary's page glows. A hair, blond or maybe silver, lies trapped between pages like a filament. I close the book and hold it to my sternum. My heart beats against it like a fist against a door.

I mean to get up and hide it again, somewhere deeper and cleverer, where Stuart won't think to search and where Mrs. Lennox won't dare disturb. But my body refuses. I tuck the diary under the pillow instead, a child's logic I can't shake. If it is near my skull the truth will leach through bone and into my thinking. If it is near my ribs the courage will travel on my blood.

I finally fall asleep again, but in the last half-waking moment, I feel, or I imagine, fingers pressing the blanket smooth along my shin, the way a mother does to tuck a child. The touch is neither gentle nor cruel but practiced. Morning will bring denial. I will tell myself I got up without remembering, that grief and terror make sleepwalkers of us all. But in the dark hours I know the diary did not climb onto my lap by itself. And I know the room wants me to keep reading. Whether that wanting is Isobel's, or the lodge's, or my own cowardice looking for permission, I can't yet say. The only thing I am certain of is the echo in my chest after the words I belong only to him. I have said something like that. I have meant it. I have let it be said to me like a vow. And now the vow tastes like iron on my tongue.

"Did you die here?" I dream-whisper one more time, into a room that will not answer.

~

The west wing is colder than the rest of the house, as if the radiators have decided their heat is wasted there. Dust lies on the runner in a soft nap that remembers every step. Cobwebs lace the corners of the high windows where frost has painted feathers on the inside of the panes. Even the portraits here are different, as though they are less certain of themselves, their paint darkened, the eyes farther away.

I tell myself I'm walking to warm my legs, to escape the Blue Suite's perfume, to keep from thinking about the diary. It is almost noon. Stuart has gone with a gamekeeper to check traps. That's his word, but in my head they are snares. The girls are upstairs in their room building a fortress out of pillows and disobedience. Mrs. Lennox disappears when he does, as if the house swallows her, and only usually reappears fully formed when he calls.

There is a corridor off the second landing that I have not taken before. It bends in a way that makes no sense, as if the wing was added by a builder who was drunk or grieving. The light grows thinner the deeper I go. I pass a door painted the gray of ashes, its handle cold in a way that feels unfriendly.

And then I see a different door. This one is not painted. Its timber is raw and dark. A padlock sits in a horseshoe of iron fixed to the jamb, its body fat and black with age. The whole thing looks theatrical, like a prop designed to tell you there is a secret behind here, and yet the feeling coming off it is not theater at all. It is warning.

I stand with my hand half lifted and feel that ridiculous nimble fear I've had since childhood that the door will choose that moment to open on its own.

"Mrs. Lennox?" I call softly, not because I want her but because the room seems to ask for a chaperone. She materializes almost at once, which should terrify me more than it does. She must have been in the linen closet behind me, or perhaps the walls actually do keep a pocket sewn for her to climb in and out. Her hands are empty. She isn't carrying a duster or a basket or a key or sheets. It's the emptiness that makes me think she knew where I was headed.

She stops when she sees which door I am studying. The color drains from her face so completely it shows me her youth for a second, the girl she used to be staring at the same iron shape.

"Best not to go in there," she says. Her voice is rougher than usual, the crisp edge gone, as if the words scrape her on their way out.

I force a small laugh. "It's locked anyway."

"Then it means to keep." The old phrase lands between us like a superstition and a law.

"What is it?" I ask. "Storage?"

I know better even as I say it. The dust on the runner records almost nothing. No crates coming and no trunks going. This door is not for things. It is for memory. Mrs. Lennox's gaze flicks to my shoulder, a servant's old trick to avoid meeting a mistress's eye without appearing insolent.

"Some doors are meant to stay closed," she murmurs.

"Why?"

The word comes out sharp and cold, and reveals that I am not just curious, I am desperate for answers to the endless questions the lodge poses. She doesn't answer. The silence yokes a story to its back. I have a sudden vivid impression of her as a young woman pressed against this same wall while voices inside the padlocked room break themselves. She takes a single step backward.

"Come away, madam," she says. She has called me Ellen before. "Please."

The please breaks something in me. I reach for her hand without meaning to, but she flinches as if I've tried to burn her. Then she curtsies, which is an absurd reflex, turns, and goes. She hurries the way someone rushes from a graveyard at dusk when they've just remembered the superstition about walking too slowly past the names of the dead.

I stay. The padlock pulses on the door like a second heart. The corridor lists slightly, it's floorboards uneven. The house is so old there is almost nothing level. I lean closer. The wood smells old, a faint hidden damp that has never been given air. I think of Isobel's entry. 'If there is a mercy it is snow. It covers and covers.' And I feel, with a clarity that makes my body go cold inside my skin, that whatever is behind this door has been covered, too. Deliberately.

I should go. I should take Mrs. Lennox's superstition like medicine and leave the west wing to rot in peace. But my feet move forward again on their own, an inch, two, the way a tongue goes searching for a sore tooth. I press my ear to the door and hold my breath. Nothing. The quiet is absolute in a way the rest of the lodge never is. It feels engineered. The lock is not there to keep someone out, my body thinks without wanting to, it is there to keep everything in.

I hear footsteps approaching behind me. They're not hurried or even heavy. They have a rhythm that implies confidence and clean soles. I pull back from the door and the motion feels like stepping away from a confession.

"That door is not your concern," Stuart says mildly.

I turn then because I have practiced the face I must wear. It's one of innocent curiosity. The trembling white flag of a woman who is easily shepherded.

"I got lost," I say, and try to smile.

He looks at the padlock like a priest looks at a relic in danger of desecration. He puts his hand to the iron as if testing its temperature and in that touch, there is possession but also something like affection. He doesn't look at me when he speaks.

"She must never know."

The pronoun slices between us. I don't have to ask which she he means. The house supplies its chorus. Isobel. She must never know. About what? About whom? His gaze lifts to me at last. The softness he wore in the study when he told me about the piano music is gone. What's left is the clean edge of control.

"This wing is shut," he says. "Do not wander here again."

I do something I have learned to do well. I lower my eyes and nod.

"Of course."

We stand there for one heartbeat too long, the way people stand in front of a coffin after the service when they cannot make themselves leave because leaving converts grief into something more permanent. Then he turns and walks me back the way I came, his hand light at my elbow, the pressure never increasing, but the intent never in doubt.

I feel the corridor bend with us. I feel the temperature rise as the west wing releases me. I feel the diary, though it is upstairs under my pillow, like a warm coin in my pocket. When we reach the second landing, he lets his fingers slip from my sleeve. He smiles the small, approving smile he gives when I have passed a test he does not tell me he set.

At supper he calls the girls "my doves" and asks Sophie about her fortress and compliments Amelia on the evenness of her handwriting. His politeness has always been more frightening than his temper. It covers so much.

Later, in the Blue Suite, when he kisses my forehead and tells me to sleep, I keep my eyes open until he does. I listen to his breath thicken and even out. When I am sure, I slide the diary out and press it flat on my lap in the dark like a map. My hands hover over it. I imagine the padlocked door, the sour smell from within, the way Mrs. Lennox said please.

Some doors are meant to stay closed. Some doors are men who build houses around their mothers and call it devotion. Behind at least one door in this lodge is a truth that begins with Isobel and ends with me if I am not careful.

"She must never know," he said.

Too late, I think. I know there is a door. I know it is locked. I know I am not meant to ask why. And knowing is the crack.

16

He leaves just after ten, the crunch of tires on old snow fading down the drive until the forest swallows the sound. I watch from the Blue Suite window as the car becomes a black punctuation mark, then nothing at all. Mrs. Lennox told him the village grocer had set aside a rare delivery of decent coffee. He said it was an errand worth the road. He kissed my forehead with the soft press he uses when he wants to make a command feel like a kindness.

"Rest," he said. "Or read."

I don't rest. And I don't read. I wait until the house has settled into its daytime routine and then I go to the dressing table. The hairpins are in a small dish beside the mirror, a few bent into commas by careless fingers. I take two and slide them inside my sleeve. The mirror gives me back a face I barely recognize, of a woman who has learned to move soundlessly in her own life.

The west wing is colder even in daylight. Dust rides the light the way moths do after dusk. I pass the ash-gray door and the dark portrait of a Drummond cousin whose eyes refuse to align.

The padlocked door is where I left it, patient and sure of itself, the lock black and heavy as if it is proud of doing its job.

I look behind me. There's nothing there. I kneel, and feel the cold of the floor striking up through my tights. The iron padlock has a faint oily film from years of hands and winter. My palms sweat anyway. I bend the first pin at the end the way I've seen in movies. Rachel once joked she could open her landlord's conscience with a bobby pin and I wish now I'd asked her to teach me something useful. I slide the bent pin into the keyway, feel the metal teeth of the cylinder like a mouth full of secrets.

The second pin becomes the turning tool. My hands shake. I force myself to breathe in fours the way I used to when Sophie was a newborn and cried like a siren for no reason I could fix. The first attempt is useless. The second scrapes, catches on nothing. The third makes a sound like a tiny cluck of metal greeting metal. I adjust, listening for small differences the way you listen for a child's breath, the way you listen for your own name in a crowded room.

Was that a footstep? I go still so completely that my heartbeat feels obscene. The corridor only creaks back at me. I push gently, coaxing, not forcing. Something shifts. The lock has character, and it doesn't want to be hurried. The fourth try finds a pin which lifts and drops like a sigh. The fifth, another. The sixth sticks so stubbornly I bite the inside of my cheek hard enough to taste iron. "Please," I whisper to a thing that cannot hear me.

It hears. Or I imagine it does. The final pin sets with a click so small it might be imagined. I turn the second clip. Resistance, then a slow, smooth give, and at last the belly-deep sound I didn't realize I craved. The padlock yields like a throat clearing after a long silence. I slide it free. My hands are shaking so hard the lock knocks the wood with a fat, dull clunk. I wince and stand, pressing it into my pocket. The door gives with a sticky reluctance, the paint on the jamb unsticking from wood like old skin. Cold air spills out, denser than the corridor's. It smells awful. Sweet yet sour, the memory of something floral rotted down into sugar and vinegar.

The room has no business being that preserved. Light comes from a narrow window glazed over with frost, enough to render the shape of a bed, larger than a single but smaller than the Blue Suite's, with an iron frame painted white long ago and yellowed to the color of teeth. The sheets are rumpled, truly rumpled, not arranged to seem so, with a nightgown laid along the center like it would be if the body had evaporated and left only the garment. The cotton has a life of its own, the shape of sleep still pressed into it. I cannot tell if I am seeing a moment frozen or one re-created so carefully that the present has dressed itself as the past.

On the floor, a perfume bottle lies shattered, the glass scattered into petals, the liquid once amber now blackened into sticky patches that has clung to the boards, then cured. If I kneel and bring my face close, the smell is unbearable, like violets turned to vinegar, a funeral bouquet left too long in a hot room. A moth, dead and perfect, is stuck in the varnish like a punctuation mark.

The walls are bare except for a single portrait. It isn't the salon's grand oil of Isobel crowned with a halo of light, but a smaller canvas in a simple frame, far more intimate. She looks out not with the serenity of the official likeness but wet-lashed, wrecked by nights of no sleep and then made to pose anyway. Her eyes are dark in that way eyes get when they have been crying too long to cry more. The painter has given her a mouth that could be pleading or blaming. In this light it is both.

My stomach folds itself into a fist. The room is still. The air doesn't move right. I try to pull a breath and it feels like unrolling gauze in my chest, yards and yards and none of it enough to bind the wound. I go to the window and press my fingers to the frost. The pane is painted shut. Someone has sealed this air in with intention.

At the bedside there is a candlestick with a wick burned low, a coin of wax dried on the sheet where a drip fell and never got picked away. On the nightstand, a tumbler with a ring of residue in it, brown and faint. The water line has a smudge that might be dust, might be the ghost of a hand. The pillow bears a shallow oval where a head once lay and, at the edge, fabric worn thin, threads popped where friction was repeated.

There is no blood. Of course, there is none. Whatever happened here wants to be named by absence. I crouch and slide my fingers beneath the bedframe. Cold dust kisses my knuckles, and cobweb threads confess themselves across my skin. My hand hits a small resistance. I pull out a ribbon, dried and brittle. It cracks as I open it. A strand of hair is caught in the knot. Not gray, but pale, the color of wheat left out all winter. It could be nothing. It could be everything.

"Mrs. Lennox?" I whisper in my mind, not meaning to.

My body answers by stepping toward the door to check the corridor, but I am a beat too late. She is already there, a tray in her hands, stacked with folded towels that slide and clatter to the floor when she sees the door open. The sound is small, but in this wing, it is a cymbal crash. We stare at each other. For a second we are two women on a frozen pond, both knowing where the thin ice is and pretending we don't.

Her lips pale as the color drains from her face. The tray hangs crooked from one hand. Then, against everything I expect, she doesn't scold. She steps inside with me just far enough that the corridor cannot hear and whispers, raw and fierce.

"Don't ever let him know."

My throat goes tight. I nod so hard my neck aches. She crouches, gathering the towels with shaking fingers.

"You shouldn't be here," she says without looking up. It sounds less like an order than like grief. "You don't want these pictures in your head."

I point toward the bed before I can stop myself. "Was this where...?" The question snags on my teeth. "Did she...?"

"Some doors are meant to stay closed," Mrs. Lennox says, louder, as if reciting a chant. But under her breath, so low I feel it more than hear it, comes the rest. "He keeps the room the way it was to test himself. Or to punish himself. I never knew which."

Punish. Test. The words buzz like a fly against glass.

"What happened, Mrs. Lennox?"

Her eyes lift to mine then, and what I see makes my knees go watery. Not fear but resignation. The look of a woman who has told truths once and been taught better. She presses the last towel to her chest.

"I will lose my place," she says simply. "Or worse. Now go."

She rushes out in a flurry of linen and hush. For a heartbeat I stand rooted, the bed, the bottle, the accusing portrait all making a triangulation that pins me in the center. I cannot bear another second of that air. I cross to the door.

The house has gone quiet in a new way. Not the daytime hush, but a listening hush. From the far end of the corridor comes a sound that doesn't belong to this wing, yet. A boot heel that knows it has a right to be anywhere. A click. The kind a key makes when it wants to be heard. I freeze. My body maps its own alibis. I slip back from the threshold, pressing myself into the slice of space behind the door and the wall, a child's trick. But he is faster than my fear.

Stuart's figure glides past the bend, blotting the far light, and appears in the doorway. For a second his face is all absence.

Bloodless and sculpted, the expression people wear when the doctor gives them words that rearrange their organs. Then his eyes register the open room, the bed, the smashed bottle, and the expression hardens in a way that makes the air colder. I step out because to hide now would be to confess something beyond trespass. I open my mouth to say I was lost. The room itself refuses the lie. The words die.

"I..." I begin.

His gaze cuts to me with surgical accuracy, and I see the exact moment it finds the shadow of the diary in my eyes, the question in my mouth, the smell of this room haunting my clothes. The pale drains from his skin and what remains is iron and steel. He steps over the threshold. He doesn't shout.

The slam of the door is shout enough, the sound so sudden and absolute it drives a flurry of dust from the curtain and snuffs whatever poor breath had been moving in here. He turns the key with a motion that is old, practiced, and final. A ritual often repeated. The lock answers him like a dog that has learned only one command.

"You had no right." His voice is low, stripped down to something that belongs in a church or a courtroom.

He crosses the room in two long strides and grips my shoulders. His hands are not the gentle, instructive ones that tilt my chin or arrange my posture. They are clamps. The pain is immediate as his thumbs dig into the soft meat below my collarbones, fingers digging into the tendons at the back.

"I told you," he says, his mouth close enough that I feel the words on my cheek, "This door was closed to you."

My body wants to say I'm sorry. It wants to unspool apology until I am a skein on the floor he can wind back onto the spindle of our life. But something else stands up inside me instead, ragged and small and stubborn.

"I needed to know," I whisper. "Not because I wanted to

betray you. Because I wanted to understand what this house did to her. What it..."

"What she did to this house," he snaps, and there is the break in the theology he never admits. That her ghost runs him, that love poured over everything he is until it calcified. "You are not ready for what this house holds."

"I am your wife," I say, and even as I say it, I hear the hollowness. He doesn't want a wife, he wants an altar.

His grip tightens until my vision pricks with whiteness.

"You are mine," he says, and the way he says mine is not the warm oath it was at first. It is a fence driven into frozen ground.

I glance at the bed because I cannot help it. The nightgown lies where a body should be. The pillow's threads gape. The broken bottle glints at the edge of my vision. My stomach moves as if it means to reject everything I've ever eaten, but there is nothing to reject. The house has been feeding me absence.

"What happened here?" I hear myself ask. I think I whisper it, but the question's shape is so large it fills the room.

He hears the shape and answers it the way he answers all things that threaten his priesthood. With doctrine.

"She was ill," he says. "She was fragile. She refused to be so strong. This room is my remembrance of her weakness." His eyes flare. "And my refusal to allow it again."

"Did she..." I can't bring myself to say die here. The words feel like a door I cannot afford to open. "Were you with her?"

"Always," he says. It is not an answer. It is a possession.

His hands lift from my shoulders as if he remembers the marks they will leave. They come back different, flattened and smoothing, the way a man calms a horse he's just spooked with his own temper. He steadies his voice.

"Listen to me. The world out there will tell you stories. The people in the village, they poison what is pure because they don't have it. This room is ours alone. Mine and hers. Now mine and yours."

"My..." My throat closes around the syllable. The thought of being kept in a room arranged like a deathbed is enough to make my knees threaten to fold.

He sees the revulsion and misnames it fear. He takes my face in his hands and forces my eyes to his.

"If you betray my trust again," he says quietly, cleanly, the way a surgeon says breathe in before he cuts. "You'll regret it."

There's a part of me that is stupid with hope and wants that to mean a lecture, a withdrawal of privileges, another night in the cabin. The dark, adult part knows better. Regret here is not a feeling. It is a process. It is a method a man learns in a house where doors have locks and locks have silence behind them.

"Do you understand?" he says.

I nod because nodding keeps the air moving. The room seals tighter around us, agreement used as mortar. He releases my face and turns away. The switch from fury to order is more frightening than the fury itself. He picks up a copper dustpan from the corner and begins, with meticulous care, to collect the shards of the perfume bottle as if the catastrophe happened yesterday and must finally be tidied. Each piece rings against the metal with the smallest chime. I think stupidly of church again, of a man ringing a bell to bring a congregation to heel. I back toward the bed to get out of his way, then stop because I refuse to give the memory of a body my shadow to lie under. The portrait watches. In this light her mouth now looks like blame.

He sets the dustpan on the dresser and wipes his hands on a handkerchief he produces from his pocket. The gesture is as intimate as anything he's ever done to me because of how practiced it is. He turns and studies the room with the eye of a curator. Then he looks at me, and whatever is on my face makes his jaw jump.

"Do not," he says, each letter clipped. "Become like the villagers."

The villagers. Moira's voice threads the crack under the door of my memory. She didn't just die. The room pitches, not physically but morally. I steady my hand on the iron bedrail because something must hold me in the present or I will bleed out into this house.

"We're done here," he says.. The door opens into that thinner air of the corridor. The world beyond this room smells of old wool and polish, which feels like mercy compared to what breathes in here. He stands aside as if he is a gentleman offering me the way. There is only one way. I pass him. His hand settles on the back of my neck, not a squeeze or a caress, but more like a reminder. He follows close enough that I feel his breath on my hair. Once we are in the corridor, he pulls the door tight and threads the lock through the iron hasp with a care that makes me sick. The padlock shuts with a sound that lands in my stomach.

He pockets the key. He smooths the doorframe with his palm as if sealing a crack with his body heat. When he looks at me, his face has rearranged itself into the tender, grave mask he wears for outsiders.

"You are not ready," he repeats, and there is something almost sorrowing in it, as if he regrets the limits of my strength like a craftsman regretful of a material that will not hold the shape he asks.

I want to spit. I want to tear the portrait off the wall and force him to look at the accusing mouth until the paint flakes in his eyes. I do neither. I stand very still and breathe like a woman listening for wolves.

We walk back through the west wing together. At the landing he loosens his hand from my neck like a favor. He says, in his gentlest voice, "Go to the Blue Suite. Rest."

I go because going is what keeps him from gripping my shoulders again. In the mirror over the dressing table, I see the marks already rising in oval bruises where his fingers wrote their names. In other lives I would cover them. Here I stare. Evidence, my mind says. Memorial, my heart answers. Warning, says whatever is left that still loves me.

17

Sunday comes thin and white, like a winter morning that looks crisp from a distance but cuts the skin up close. The lodge is even quieter than usual, as if even the pipes keep Sabbath. Stuart stands in the doorway of the Blue Suite while I pull on my boots. He has already tied the scarf at my throat himself. It's too tight. The knot feels like a small hand gripping my neck.

"Service," he says, like the word might wash me. "Mrs. Lennox will accompany you." The sentence wears the decoration of permission, but the metal beneath is custody.

Mrs. Lennox waits in the mudroom with her hat pinned at a precise angle, gloves matched to the wool at her sleeves. She doesn't meet my eye as we step out into the white. The snow squeaks underfoot in a sharp, clean complaint. Breath lifts from our mouths like the afterthoughts of prayers.

The car leaves us at the village church where the steeple looks like a finger tapering into the sky. The bell fumbles its way through the hour, reluctant. Inside, the space is small and close and warm, heated by a single iron stove at the back. Men stamp snow from boots. Women strip off gloves finger by finger and tuck them into their sleeves like secret animals. Children are arranged, corrected, hushed.

We sit three rows from the back, as if there's a rule about where the lodge sends its people so that we are visible, but not too seen. I feel the look of the congregation like a draft. Some are curious, some wary, one or two soft with pity they tuck away when they remember themselves. Mrs. Lennox kneels with the thin, practiced economy of a body that has been bowing all its life. When she rises, her mouth shapes a hymn without sound.

The minister speaks of wilderness and testing, of manna and obedience, of the way God brings His beloved into the desert to teach them dependence. My throat tightens. I never learned the language of church except the American kind, of potlucks and casseroles and sung comfort. This is something else. This is a sermon sharpened into a spear. Every time he says house, my ribs ache. Every time he says father, the skin between my shoulder blades crawls.

Moira O'Donnell sits two pews up, her hat practical, her coat buttoned all the way despite the warmth of the stove. She doesn't turn, not once, but when the congregation bows their heads, she keeps hers a fraction higher, and that small refusal is a flare I want to run toward.

After the benediction, the aisle becomes a corridor of hands and murmurs. I feel like a girl in a school line, expected to move, to smile the correct amount, to let myself be carried along by other people's intentions. Outside, the churchyard glitters with fresh crust, sun collapsing in cold shards off the graves. Small stones wear white caps. Names sleep beneath them in old alphabets.

Mrs. Lennox takes my elbow and steers me down the path toward the gate. Our breath ghost-pairs behind us on the wind. "Straight to the car," she murmurs, as if a different route could change the weather of my life.

That is when Moira appears at my other side, as if she has always walked there, like a third echo. She doesn't touch me. She walks exactly parallel, a half step behind, as though we are three women linked by a thread we've each agreed not to tug.

"Mrs. Drummond." Her voice is pitched for the path, not the pews. "It's so good to see you." A civil greeting anyone could hear. Her eyes, though, slide to mine with a charge that snaps like dry pine.

"Mrs. O'Donnell." I manage the small talk shape of her name without turning my head. Mrs. Lennox's hand tightens, just once, like a warning squeeze through the wool.

Moira's voice glances off the air between us, innocuous to anyone not listening for the grain under the varnish.

"The winter has a way of clarifying things, doesn't it? You can almost see the shape of what's buried." She lowers her lashes as we slip past a drift grown into a small cliff. "Stuart's allowing you out, then."

Allowing. The word pricks me, both small and accurate. Before I can answer, she exhales a little laugh with too much edge for humor.

"I'll be plain. There isn't much time to pretend at niceties. Isobel's death was not natural."

The churchyard is suddenly all ears and stone. My boots misjudge a ridge. I slide, correct my step, feel my ankle cry out and quiet itself.

"What do you mean," I say, but it isn't a question. It is a door.

"She wasted away," Moira says. "People like to make it poetic. It wasn't. She thinned out and slowed and then she was gone. Some say poison, or a tonic mixed wrong or on purpose, who can know? Some say she did it to herself because that was the only way to leave him. Enough whisper it that the whisper has roots."

"Mrs. O'Donnell." Lennox's voice is papercut-sharp. "You are overstepping."

Moira doesn't look at her.

"And some say her last weeks were kept under lock. Visitors forbidden. Servants sent home. That house swallows witnesses and then claims there were none." Her hand moves, only a fraction, only the smallest flick of wrist, and something light is pressed into my glove. Paper, folded tight into a square, carrying the warmth from her palm. I keep walking. I don't look down. The paper is a moth beating its quiet wings in my hand.

"She will be late for the car," Mrs. Lennox says to the air, to me, to the world, as if the complaint is an incantation. "We don't keep Mr. Drummond waiting."

Moira's mouth tilts.

"No," she says, and the single syllable is loaded with knowledge, sympathy, and contempt in even thirds. At the gate she lets herself tip a step ahead so that for a heartbeat we're side by side, breathing the same shocked air. Her voice drops, a ribbon in the snow's ear.

"He will never let you go."

The phrase is not news, and yet it strikes like a fall through ice. Like a cold shock, or the breath-losing truth of a thing you didn't have the courage to name yourself. I feel the letter pulse once against my palm, like a small, secret animal. I nod, not because I agree, but because my neck doesn't know how else to move.

"Thank you," I whisper, so softly the wind steals it and leaves my mouth empty.

Moira nods once in that brisk way people do when the hard part is saying the thing and the second-hard part is not saying more.

"You'll know when to read it," she whispers. Then she is

gone, drawn toward another cluster of wool and steam breath, absorbed back into town like a drop of water into snow.

The car idles by the hedge, its exhaust making little ghosts that vanish fast. Mrs. Lennox opens the door for me with hands that tremble and then hold absolutely still.

"If I were a different sort of woman," she says without looking at me, "I would have stopped you taking that. I am not, it seems."

She shuts the door carefully, as if closing a child into a room to keep her safe, and goes around to her side without another word. On the drive back the paper in my glove starts to feel hot, then unbearably obvious. I tuck it into my sleeve and pretend to sleep so I don't spend the whole trip looking at her profile and asking whether she is ally or audit. The trees pass like tall black lines painted in a hurry. When the lodge appears, it looks superimposed on the sky, as if it has forgotten that other houses are supposed to keep neighbors. Mrs. Lennox squeezes my wrist once before we climb the steps, her eyes forward. It could be a warning. It could be a blessing. It could be both.

Stuart is waiting in the hall, coat still on, gloved, as if the act of missing me even for church has made him restless.

"How was it?" he asks, a husband's question borrowed from better men and turned into surveillance.

"Quiet," I say, and the truth is in it.

His smile is small and satisfied. "Good. Reflection suits you." He unties my scarf and reknots it looser as if kindness were a trophy he can pin to himself. The letter rides my pulse under my cuff like a live thing. I keep my hands at my sides. I keep my eyes where he wants them. I swallow the urge to run upstairs, and let a stranger's words change the temperature of my body. He dismisses us with a touch to my shoulder and a nod to Mrs. Lennox.

"Lunch," he says into the air, and the air obeys.

I hang my coat. I count my breaths in fours. I do not let myself look down until I'm alone behind the Blue Suite door with the perfume and the tracked shadows of Isobel's skirts. Only then do I slide the square from my sleeve and feel the heat of the church's stove trapped in its folds. Only then do I unknot my glove from my hand and hold the paper like skin.

You will know when to read it. I put the square under the pillow and sit on the bed with my coat still on, and for a long time I do nothing but listen to the lodge breathe, deciding when night will be dark enough to open it and if any of it will still belong to me in the morning.

The house loosens its jaw after midnight. I lie with my coat beside me and the square of paper under the pillow turned talisman. Stuart's breath slows to the rhythm I recognize, a heavy wave, with a minor catch, the unconscious sound a man makes when he believes no one can leave him. When I am sure he's asleep, I slide out from under the covers and cross to the window to use the thin seam of snow-reflected light. I sit on the floor with my back against the bed. The paper opens with a dry-boned little cry.

Moira's hand is quick and tidy, the script of a woman who learned penmanship when it still mattered. It isn't long, just two pages only, but it contains more detail than the room or the time will allow me. I read once, scanning it quickly, and have to go back, this time letting each sentence settle like ash.

Ellen, it begins. She uses my first name as if our acquaintance were permission enough. When I told you there were whispers, I didn't mean the kind that go in circles for sport. I mean the kind people only say with the curtains drawn.

I can see her at her kitchen table writing, her jaw set. I can see the stove painting the edges of the paper with warmth.

The cook before last, Nora, came to me one winter once her hands stopped shaking and her mouth remembered water. She said the west wing was closed those weeks. She said the master, your father-in-law, turned the key himself and carried it in his pocket like a charm. He forbade callers and sent the maids home early if they crossed the landing. He told the post to leave parcels at the drive. He sent the doctor away the last time with a smile you would not want pointed at you.

I breathe. I hear the lock. I hear the way a key speaks when it knows it is important.

She said the lady faded. That is the word she used, and I asked three times if she meant hunger or illness, and she put both hands flat on my table and said, "Moira, both." The lady would not eat and the things she did swallow didn't stay down. The bottles were labeled tonic and sleeping draft. One smelled sharp like medicine, one sweet like sugar gone bad.

The shattered bottle in the locked room throws its ghost-smell at my face. The moth trapped in resin. The sticky dark that used to be amber.

Some say poison. You hear all sorts. Like arsenic from flypaper boiled into water, laudanum liberally poured, a husband who thinks removing appetite is another kind of pruning. I cannot tell you that truth. I can tell you Nora swore her soul she saw the boy, you know which, sit outside a locked door with his hands clasped in prayer like a statue. She said he was there at all hours you would not wish on a child. She said he would tell anyone who paused that his mother was sleeping and needed quiet, and he said it like a prayer he was trying to make work by saying it right.

I stop and press my knuckle to my mouth. The picture arrives ready-made of a small Stuart in the corridor, jaw set the way it is now, inventing a vigil he could keep because he could not fight the man who held the key. The phrase idolizing her decline arrives unsummoned and refuses to leave. He has learned to love the slope away as a holy curve.

Later, Moira writes, when the undertaker had done what undertakers do and the house returned to the sound it makes when it thinks it is empty, the staff were called back and the room was closed. Closed is a generous word. Locked is the right one. The bedding was not washed. A maid with sense would tell you that means grief. A maid with a different kind of sense would tell you that means something else. I am both kinds of woman and have learned the usefulness of each.

The nightgown laid out as if the body might remember itself. The pillow's threads gaped by worry. The coin of wax set like a date.

I tell you this because I watched you in the store and later in the church, and I know the look of a woman being remade into a different role. Do not let them keep you in that shape. He will call it love. He will call it purity. He will call it family. Survival is not a sin.

Her hand is not neat on that last sentence. The ink bites a little deeper, as if the nib cried.

One last thing, the letter says on the second page, the words smaller. There are records. Not the kind that sit where men can find them and gloat. Women's records. The laundress wrote dates in soap on the inside of a cupboard door when she could not keep them all in her head, because she said forgetting sorrow makes it breed. The day visitors were turned away. The day the doctor did not return. The day the parlour drapes were changed for the black ones and the master said not to ask a cloth why it is dark. The cupboard is in the west wing linen press. The marks may still be there under paint.

My heart trips itself. The linen press. The west wing. A cupboard door and soap. Dates that refuse to die with the water.

I see Mrs. Lennox's hands draped in towels. I hear her please and the way it was addressed to more than me.

I do not promise safety, Moira ends. Only company. Bring the children if you run. Do not send a note. He reads paper as if it were a rival. If you cannot leave yet, learn the rooms as if they are weather. There is always a seam. He will never let you go. So, you must go without his letting.

The letter trembles in my hands and I realize it is not the paper but my bones. I fold the pages back along their creases until the paper is a small square again, and tuck it under the mattress where the seam is torn. The lodge knows every pocket I possess, so I must begin to make new ones.

I sit very still and listen to the house identify me. Wife. Mother. Replacement. Vessel. Heart. I imagine the cupboard in the press with its hidden arithmetic. I imagine soap words beneath paint like ghosts that cannot stop being honest. I imagine the corridor boy grown into a man who makes rooms into altars, who believes mourning is worship the way some men believe love is a leash. I imagine the locked door and the nightgown and the glass in the dustpan and the sound a padlock makes when it wants to be heard.

Under the pillow, the diary's spine presses back at my shoulder blade like a spine answering a spine. I pull it out and lay it across my knees, not to read but to feel the weight and tell myself that this is not a book, it is a map. It shows me a country I refuse to occupy until I die.

Beside me, Stuart turns in his sleep and exhales my name into the dark as if possession could be breathed. I watch his profile and feel something in me go hard and quiet, like water when it decides to be ice.

"Soon," I mouth, a vow stolen back from all the wrong altars. "Soon."

The cupboard with the soap dates waits in the west wing

with its door closed and its truth intact. My daughters sleep in their small fortress of quilts with their hair electric from the dry air. Moira's hand is still in the pages like heat. He will never let you go.

So, I will not ask.

18

The girls' room is the only place in the lodge that still remembers childhood. The wallpaper is faded, patched in places, and the air carries the faint, innocent smell of wax crayons even though none have been unpacked since we arrived. At night, when the rest of the house exhales its long, watching silence, this room keeps its own rhythm in the whisper of small breaths, the rustle of quilts, the occasional giggle Sophie can't quite contain before she shushes herself.

Tonight, though, there is no giggling. Only the glow of the lamp on the dresser, its flame swaying in the draft. Sophie is curled against the wall, half-asleep, thumb in her mouth, hair tangled across the pillow. Amelia sits cross-legged at the end of the bed, her face lit from below, her eyes dark pools of someone far older than ten.

"Mom." Her voice is quiet but pointed. "He's hurting you, isn't he?"

The words hang in the air, heavy as a bell toll. I open my mouth and close it again. The reflex to deny, to protect, is strong. I want to tell her everything is fine, that bruises fade, that rules are just rules. But she's looking at me with a gaze so direct it cuts through every pretense. She has seen the marks on my wrists. She has heard the way my voice falters. She has lived long enough under Stuart's roof to know what danger feels like.

I draw a breath, shaky.

"We're... we're not safe, Amelia." My voice cracks, and I reach for her hand before I can lose the courage. "You're right. He's trying to control us. All of us."

Her chin lifts in a way that makes her look suddenly older than her years.

"Then we have to do something. We can't just sit here and wait for him to break us."

The bluntness of her words makes my stomach clench. I glance toward Sophie, still half-dreaming. Her eyelids flutter, and I realize she's listening, even in that drowsy state.

"Amelia," I whisper, squeezing her hand. "He watches everything. He'll know if we try."

"Not if we're smart," she says quickly, leaning closer. "I've been thinking. The deliveries when the man brings baskets to the kitchen. Mrs. Lennox checks them but she doesn't look at every little thing. If we wrote a note, tucked it under the cloth or between the tins, someone in the village might find it. They'd know we need help."

The plan is reckless, fragile, but my heart lurches at her ingenuity. I see Michael in her stubbornness, Thomas in her precision. And me, too. The part of me that still believes survival isn't surrender.

I brush a strand of hair from her face. "It's dangerous."

Her eyes don't waver. "It's more dangerous to do nothing."

From the other bed, Sophie stirs, her small voice muffled against the pillow. "What are you talking about?"

Amelia shifts to sit beside her sister, lowering her voice but keeping the same steel. "We're going to get out, Soph. Mom and me. And you, too." She places a hand on Sophie's hair. "We just have to be careful."

Sophie's eyes widen, fear glistening. She looks at me, searching for reassurance. I crawl across the bed and gather them both into my arms. Sophie buries her face against my chest, her little fingers clutching the fabric of my sleeve. Amelia leans into me too, though her body is rigid with determination.

"We'll be smart," I whisper into their hair. "We'll try. But until the right moment comes, we have to pretend. You can't let him see your thoughts. Do you understand?"

Amelia nods. Sophie sniffles but whispers, "Okay."

I feel the weight of them pressed against me. The fragile, trusting warmth of Sophie, and the fierce, unyielding resolve of Amelia. One clings like a child, the other schemes like a woman twice her age. Both are mine. Both are counting on me. I kiss the crowns of their heads, one after the other, and vow silently that I will not let them grow up into ghosts.

~

The study feels different at night. The fire burns low, with coals glowing red like watchful eyes, shadows standing taller than the furniture that casts them. Stuart sits in his chair, one hand on the armrest, the other holding a glass he hasn't touched. His posture is easy, but his eyes are sharp and unblinking, hiding a predator's patience.

I stand in the doorway until he gestures for me to come closer. My steps feel loud on the rug, though they make no sound.

"You've been restless," he says as I sink into the chair opposite. His voice is smooth and tender, but the softness carries the edge of a blade.

"I..." My throat tightens. "It's the house. The storms. I haven't been sleeping well."

He leans forward, setting the glass aside. His hand lifts, and he strokes my hair slowly, rhythmically, like a man soothing an animal.

"You don't ever think of leaving, do you?"

The question slices through me. I keep my face still, force my eyes to meet his.

"No."

The lie feels heavy, but I dress it in the truth of my tone. His thumb brushes my temple, his touch gentle but his gaze scorching.

"Without me, you are nothing," he murmurs, the words sliding under my skin. "Without you, I am nothing. We belong to each other, always."

My heart hammers against my ribs. He says it like a vow, but it lands like a sentence. A tether tightening, pulling the air from my lungs. I nod, because nodding is safer than silence.

"Always," I whisper.

His smile blooms, faint and satisfied. He withdraws his hand, sits back in his chair. The fire pops, sending a spark skittering up the chimney.

"You see," he says softly. "Strength lies in devotion. There is no need for doubt. Doubt poisons. But you..." His eyes fix on me, gleaming. "You are strong."

The words are meant to soothe, but my stomach twists. I hear Moira's warning. He will never let you go. I hear Amelia's fierce whisper. It's more dangerous to do nothing. Both voices clang inside me, colliding with his doctrine until I feel dizzy with the noise. I force a smile.

"I understand."

"Good." His voice softens further, almost like a lullaby.

"Then rest easy. Your place is here. With me. With the girls. There is nowhere else."

I bow my head slightly in a gesture of submission that keeps the firelight from catching the defiance in my eyes. Inside, I know the truth. His obsession is no longer a chain I can learn to bear. It is a noose. And if I don't act soon, it will close around not just my throat, but Amelia's and Sophie's too. Time is running out.

19

The grandfather clock ticks in a way that feels louder than time has any business being. When the knocker thuds at the back door, the sound travels through the stone like a pulse. Mrs. Lennox is already halfway down the stairs, keyed to the rhythm of the place the way a bird knows weather before it comes.

"Provisions," she says, not because I don't know, but because saying things out loud keeps them orderly. She smooths her apron with a palm that trembles once and then goes obediently still.

I've coached the girls to boredom. "We will treat the delivery as the most boring errand in the world," I told them in a whisper last night. "As if we have done it a million times and nothing about it interests us." Amelia nodded like a captain accepting a mission she'd already mapped three ways. Sophie nodded too, then asked if being bored could be a game.

Now, as the door swings wide and a gust of wind shoulders in, Sophie's hand finds mine, small and hot in the cold. Amelia steps slightly ahead, chin lifted, the picture of a child trying to look smaller by looking bigger. The farmer has the posture of a man who has carried heavy burdens through too many winters.

He tips snow from his cap with a gloved hand and stomps once on the flagstones by reflex.

A second man, a boy, really, with chapped cheeks and hair the color of corn husk, follows with a second crate. They both smell like outdoors. Like hay, cold iron, damp wool, the sour-sweet of apples stored near potatoes.

"Weather's making a mess of the road," the farmer says, eyes flicking quickly past my shoulder into the hall, the way local men always do in this house, as if expecting it to be different and finding, to their relief or disappointment, that it is exactly the same. "But we got your list."

"Kitchen," Mrs. Lennox says, already turning. "Mind the runner."

She takes the lead like a general, and for once I'm grateful. Her movement is cover and what is rehearsed is safe. Amelia and I flank the nearest crate, not quite touching it, like acolytes to a heavy reliquary. Inside, between folded towels the farmer used as padding, lie the everyday mercies that now feel like contraband. Flour, tinned beans, onions with their skins like paper, a cluster of carrots with dirt still dried at their tips, the dull gleam of canned tomatoes, a sack of sugar tied with twine. Our note is smaller than any of it. It weighs nothing and everything.

I made the letters last night by the window, copying Amelia's careful script so that if anything in it could be traced, it would be to a woman trying to seem like a child, or a child trying to seem like a woman. Help. Drummond Lodge. Woman and two children. Phone lines dead. He won't let us go. No names. No dates. A seam along the edge where, if a person wasn't looking, it would feel like just another fold in a brown paper lining.

The kitchen is warm enough to sting. The iron stove breathes steadily, making the ceiling low with heat. The windows are fogged, and beyond them the snow drifts up the panes like the lake rising. On the table, Mrs. Lennox spreads her inventory sheets with a precision that could cut.

"Flour," she says. "One. Two." She ticks boxes with her pencil, leaves identical dark graves for every item.

"Set them here," she orders. The farmer lifts the front of the crate to clear the table edge. The boy's boots squeak on the tile and he grins nervously at the noise and looks to the farmer for permission to keep smiling. The farmer doesn't give it, he just grunts, which in this house counts as a blessing.

"Mom," Sophie whispers, tugging my sleeve. "Can I hold the apples?"

"In a minute," I say, and wish I had more minutes to hand her.

Mrs. Lennox bends to check the weight of the sugar. Her back is to us. It's the only space Amelia needs. She moves like quiet water. Her hand slides along the lip of the crate, fingers groping between the bottom slat and the thin paper the farmer used to keep the carrots from bruising. For an instant I see the square of our note as a pale flicker against the darker wood. Then Amelia's hand is empty again. She is straightening a towel. She is ten years old and the towel must be tidy, everyone knows that.

Mrs Lennox's voice cuts over to her, loud in the room.

"What are you doing?"

"Counting," Amelia says quickly, as though it's perfectly obvious. She taps two carrots with a nail. "Two. Three. Four. If there's four carrots we win."

Sophie considers. "We win what?"

"Cake. If there's four carrots, it means there's cake in the future." Amelia's voice is a steady thread. She doesn't look at me. She doesn't need to. I follow her through the needle's eye like I've been doing it all my life.

"Four," Sophie repeats, solemn now, as if she himself has

been sworn into a cult. She counts under her breath. One, two, three, four, and beams, the simple arithmetic saving us because it looks like what childhood ought to look like.

"Cake," she whispers, and the word is the first prayer I believe in this house.

"Sugar," Mrs. Lennox says again, pencil pausing. "That's a full sack?"

"As ordered," the farmer answers. His voice has the dryness of a man who has learned not to say more than he needs to in these rooms. His eyes skip around the kitchen, landing briefly, gently, on each of us, the girls, me, before he drops them, the way a person drops their gaze at open casket out of respect for the living who must walk past it.

"Coffee," Mrs. Lennox says, and the word perks even the air. The boy produces a brown packet from the second crate like a magician offering proof of magic. "Hard to get," he says, almost proud. The farmer huffs.

My heart counts its own inventory. The note, hidden. The weight of Stuart's absence. The distance into town. The number of minutes this moment can survive if pressed. I force my hands to move in ordinary ways. I lift an onion and feel its papery skin shed a little on my palm. I untie the twine on the sugar and peek inside like a woman who cares about freshness. My head nods. My mouth makes appreciative shapes. My body is a costume I put on for the house's benefit.

"Sign," Mrs. Lennox says, sliding the sheet forward in a neat square. She holds the pencil out to me, the way a teacher offers forgiveness by giving a child another chance.

My signature looks like a person who is not me. It's smaller, a hair pinched between two fingers.

"There now," the farmer says. He tips his cap to Mrs. Lennox, to me, and to the stove, which in this winter qualifies as a person you ought to thank. The boy hefts the empty crate, grin returning now that the warm part is over, the part with women and lists and wells of something he can't name. They go, the door lets in one last complaint of cold, then shuts. The kitchen exhales. We are still. I don't know I've been holding my breath until my body demands air like a debt collector. I cough softly into my cuff and the sound sounds like a woman who is tired, which is a true enough lie.

Mrs. Lennox finishes her tick marks, stacks the sheets, closes the ledger with a small, satisfied thump. She won't look at me. She won't look at Amelia. That not-looking is its own gaze, monumental. As she turns to the pantry with the sack of sugar against her chest, she says, casually, to no one, "Funny how paper finds its way where it is needed."

My heart skips, then hammers triple time.

"Yes," I say, as if we are talking about sugar.

"Will there be cake?" Sophie demands, tugging at my sleeve again, mission accomplished.

"If there is any justice left in this house," I say, and the words make Amelia's eyes flash with something like a laugh she does not dare emit.

By the time the clock scolds the hour again, the front hall has returned to its old silence, the wet on the flagstones drying to nothing, the scent of hay loosened into the air like a story someone told only once. I press the girls' hair flat as they run down the corridor. I let my palm rest a second longer on Amelia's crown.

"Good," I whisper. The word is so small it can hide in her curls. "Good."

But already another sound has begun to knit itself out of the quiet, a note I have learned to hear beneath other notes of the house preparing to report back on our behavior.

For the rest of the morning a flicker lives under my ribs in the shape of paper traveling out into the world. I cling to the thought like a talisman. Someone might read the plea. Someone might come. The road may be bad, the weather may be worse, but words can cross where wheels cannot. If the farmer finds it when he unloads, if the boy sees it when he wipes out the crate, if anyone in that warm store can be more than sorry, then the lodge, for once, will not have the last word.

I hold that thought like heat between my hands until it threatens to burn me.

~

He summons me at dusk, just as the snow gives up the pretense of falling straight and starts to drift in sideways sheets. The study door is open. The fire is newly fed, flames bright enough to throw the portraits into sharp relief. They look more alive when the light flickers, making their eyes shine as if they have been weeping in oil.

"Close it," he says without turning, and something inside me hunches before I've even obeyed. The latch settles softly, like a small animal curling into itself.

He stands at the desk with his back to me, one hand flat on the wood, the other holding something between two fingers the way a man might hold a cigarette he does not intend to smoke. He doesn't speak for a long count of three, two, one, and then he turns.

The folded square is unmistakable. Not opened or stained. Not even wet from snow. Exactly as it left my fingers and found my daughter's, and hers found the dark between crate and paper lining. The sight of it here, in his hand, slackens my knees for a half breath.

"So," he says. The word is gentle and terrible. "You've been plotting."

The room shrinks. The fire snaps in a way that sounds like a laugh covered quickly with a cough.

"I don't..." I begin, because it's reflex, the old, stupid hope that denial can rewind a moment to before it was lived. "I don't know what that is."

He smiles, and the smile is worse than whatever other face he might have made.

"Don't lie," he says, not unkindly. He tilts the paper in his fingers as if testing its weight. "It doesn't suit you."

I say the next thing without deciding to. "It's not opened."

"No," he agrees. "It isn't." The paper taps the air twice between us, almost playful. "I didn't need to read it to know what it says. Words sent like this are always the same."

His eyes skim me, lowering, narrowing, like a man measuring drapes he plans to pull down.

"Help. Trapped. Children." He tastes the last word, rolls it in his mouth, then lets it go. "As if the world would know what to do with you if it got you."

My mind scrambles, listing explanations, excuses, all of them brittle. "Maybe it fell..."

"From a basket someone had not yet touched?" His brows lift, an actor admiring a line he's heard too often. "No. Don't cheapen yourself with poor lies."

He steps nearer. The paper looks suddenly obscene in his hand, naked where it meant to be clothed in blankets. He does not reach for me. He does not need to.

"Listen," he says, and all the warmth he gave the word at church is gone. "You will never leave me."

I try to breathe, to set my face into a shape that can survive this.

"We're a family," I murmur, because I am not ready to say prison to his face.

"A purity," he corrects. "Which you have tried to stain with town gossip and childish tricks. Notes, Ellen? Smuggled in baskets? Do you think so little of me? Of my house?"

Heat rises up my neck, shame's hot hand even when I know shame doesn't belong to me.

"I'm tired," I say, playing to the one place he lets the word live. "I've been unwell."

"You have," he agrees softly, and the softness frightens me more than anything else. "You've been infected by doubt." He lifts the note to my eye level, pinched between two fingers, a surgeon displaying a foreign object removed from an organ. "You forgot who you are without me."

"I haven't forgotten," I say, but the words sound like fog on glass.

He moves closer, until the paper disappears out of my sight and all I can see is his face, full of calm intent, the study's fire making a saint's flicker around his head that I hate, hate, hate.

"If you try again," he says, almost velvety, "I'll make sure the children pay the price."

There it is. The knife. He doesn't drive it. He just sets the edge to my throat and waits to watch me bleed myself on it. The first thought is not mine. It is animal. Hide them. Hide them. Hide them. The second is mine and it survives. Remember everything. Breathe anyway.

"What do you mean?" My voice is smaller than I want it to be. I force it to hold shape. "They're just children."

He makes a sound like pity with no pity in it.

"And children learn. They can be taught obedience in ways adults cannot. Little corrections," he says, and something in my chest turns to glass. "Privileges removed. Lessons arranged. Cold is instructive. Hunger, too. You of all people know I do not shirk the work required to shape a soul."

My hands clench so hard my nails bite my palms.

"Don't touch them," I say, and the heat I've been smothering for months flares, clean, bright, and life-giving. "Don't you dare."

His head tilts. Admiration's ghost visits his mouth and leaves.

"There she is," he murmurs. "The strength I saw." He lets the compliment sit like a fly on a glass. "Use it properly. At my side. As my heart."

He turns away then, as if the matter is settled, as if the blade has been sheathed when I can still feel it. He sets the folded note on the desk blotter and lays a paperweight over it. The sight is absurd and chilling. Our plea trapped under glass by a man who prefers his objects still. He looks back without moving his body, just his eyes, the way a portrait looks both across a room and straight at you.

"Tell Mrs. Lennox you'll need more sugar if you mean to keep the girls in cakes," he says, as if we are talking about recipes.

"You intercepted it," I hear myself say, as if naming the trick changes anything. "How?"

He smiles in a way that makes the answer unnecessary.

"Nothing enters or leaves this house without my blessing," he says. "Did you truly not understand that?" He waves a hand gently, a priest dismissing a penitent. "Go."

I don't move. The room sways almost imperceptibly, a ship in a sea of carpet. The paper lies under the weight like a flattened bird. He lifts a brow. The silence presses at my ears. The portraits approve the lesson with their old, terrible eyes.

"Go," he repeats, no louder, and I find my legs.

The corridor outside feels colder than the study, though the radiators bank heat along the baseboards. I walk without seeing until the runner catches under my heel and I nearly fall. My palms slap the wainscoting. The wood is warm from the house's breath. I wait for my heart to remember how to beat in a way that doesn't rattle.

20

The lock turns with the sound of a throat clearing, a small, final gesture. I fling myself at the door, but Stuart is already on the other side. The bolt slides into place, clean and sure.

"Stuart!" My voice is raw, ragged. "Don't you dare! Don't take them from me!"

The corridor outside carries the sound of Sophie crying, high and panicked, Amelia's voice pitched lower, but no less frantic. "Mom! Mom!"

I slam my shoulder against the wood until it jars the bone. "Bring them back! Please don't touch them!"

His reply is calm, almost pious. "They need guidance. I told you I would take care of it if you failed them."

The cries move down the hallway, thinner now, stretched by distance. I press my ear to the panel, catch a snatch of words. Stuart's voice, measured and instructing.

"Word by word, Amelia. Begin."

A pause, then my daughter's voice, trembling but clear.

"Do not go gentle into that good night."

I suck in air as though the poem itself has struck me. Isobel's favorite. Stuart recited it once in the study as if prayer and memory were the same.

"...rage, rage against the dying of the light..."

Amelia's voice falters, then stumbles deliberately. A wrong word, a misplaced phrase.

"Young lady," Stuart says, his tone tightening. "Again. With care."

My fists pound the door until my knuckles split. "She's just a child! Leave her alone!" Blood slicks my skin. My voice breaks. "It's me you want, not them!"

The Blue Suite swallows my words. The wallpaper's velvet lilies leer. Their voices fade down the corridor. He's taking them away.

"Do not," Amelia insists, her voice sharper now. "Do not go gentle..."

Sophie sobs in the background, her small cries like knives. Through the tall window I glimpse movement in the courtyard. Shadows climb the staircase built along the exterior wall toward the attic gable. Stuart's tall frame leads, the girls following, their coats thin, their bodies small against the snow. Amelia's arm is around Sophie, pulling her forward.

"No," I whisper. "No!"

I slam both fists against the window glass until pain sings through my arms. I beat the door until my palms ache. "You bastard! Give them back to me!"

Above, the gable window flares as a light flickers on in the attic. I stagger back, heart hammering, then lunge for the window again. Through the fogged glass I see shapes moving inside, small and hesitant. The attic is a room no child should ever step into. And then I realize what they're seeing.

Canvas after canvas, propped against beams, leaning in rows. Portraits of Isobel, thin, wasted, eyes ringed dark. Each one worse than the last. Her skin yellowed in oils, her lips cracked in paint. Dozens, maybe more, charting her decline stroke by stroke until she isn't luminous but cadaverous.

Sophie's little scream pierces even the glass, even over the wind. I can see them pause before a final canvas, huge, dominating the far wall. Even from here I know what it shows. The posture, the sheet, the stillness. A corpse rendered in paint. Isobel's face frozen forever in the moment after breath left her. I collapse against the door.

"God, no. Please, don't let them see that. Don't make them."

My body convulses with sobs, violent, wracking. I pound until I can't feel my hands anymore. Until I slump to the rug, bruised palms against velvet lilies, listening to my daughters' cries echo from the rafters of a house that seems like it eats children whole.

I don't know how long I stay there, but night smothers the Blue Suite. The perfume thickens. My body trembles with exhaustion, my muscles ache from hammering on the door. At some point I collapse across the bed, face pressed to the pillow where Isobel's scent lingers most. Sleep is not sleep but a fever dream. She comes to me again.

Isobel stands at the foot of the bed again, pale as frost, her eyes wells of grief. Her lips move and this time sound comes, barely a thread.

"He won't let you live."

Her voice is wind through broken glass, soft and endless.

"He won't let them live."

Her hands lift, trembling. She points, first at my chest, then toward the corridor, then upward, toward the attic, where my girls sleep tonight surrounded by her painted death.

"There's only one way out."

I jolt awake with a sob. My body is slick with sweat despite the cold. The perfume claws at me. But something inside me has shifted. Endurance has rotted away and patience has expired.

He won't let me live. He won't let them live. Only one way out. The thought chills me more than the snow creeping through the sash. But it is also clean and sharp, like a blade I can finally see.

I whisper to the darkness, to Isobel, to myself.

"I won't let him finish us."

21

The dining hall is a cathedral of shadows and fire. Candles blaze on the long oak table, their flames multiplied in the polished silver until it looks like the air itself is burning. The storm outside hurls snow against the high windows, but here inside the heat presses close, smothering.

Stuart has planned every detail. He greeted me in the Blue Suite with a dress already laid out. Its silk is the color of faded violets, so I know it's Isobel's. When I hesitated, he lifted the gown and held it open like a lover, his eyes daring me to refuse. My body obeyed before my mind had time to scream. The fabric smells faintly of dust and the cloying perfume that never leaves these walls. When he fastened the clasp at my throat, I felt the chain of it more than the silk.

Now he ushers me into the hall, his hand firm on my back. He guides me to the chair at the end of the table. Isobel's seat, I realize, not mine. The chair is taller, carved with a crown motif at its crest. When I hesitate again, he grips my shoulder, squeezing hard enough to send a jolt of pain.

"Smile," he murmurs, low enough that only I can hear. "She always smiled."

I force my lips into the shape of something that might pass for a smile, though my stomach clenches so tight I fear I might be sick across the table.

The girls are already seated. Amelia's hands are folded in her lap, her face set, her eyes blazing with the kind of fury children shouldn't have to know. She stares straight at Stuart, unblinking. Sophie sits beside her, small shoulders hunched, eyes wet. She sobs quietly, the sound muffled by her sleeve. Mrs. Lennox hovers by the sideboard, her face pale, her hands clasped in front of her like she's at a funeral. Perhaps she is.

The food is arranged in grotesque abundance. Roast meat glistening under its glaze, bowls of potatoes, carrots swimming in butter, platters of bread steaming as if just pulled from the oven. The smell is rich, heavy, and sickening.

Stuart sits opposite me, his posture perfect, and his smile gleaming. He lifts a glass, and the ruby wine catches the light like blood.

"To eternity," he declares, his voice ringing with solemn joy. "To perfection. To us."

The toast hangs in the air like incense in a poisoned chapel. I lift my glass with trembling fingers. The stem is slick with sweat. Amelia doesn't move. She keeps her glare steady on him, hands still in her lap. Sophie buries her face in her arm and sobs harder. Stuart's smile tightens. His eyes flick to Amelia, the warmth in them hardening to steel.

"Drink," he says. His voice is quiet, but it carries.

Amelia shakes her head, slow, deliberate. "No."

The tiny word cracks the air like glass breaking. My heart lurches. I half rise, terrified, but Stuart doesn't explode. He doesn't raise his voice. Instead, he leans back in his chair, his smile widening into something grotesque.

"Strong," he says, as if admiring her. "Just like your mother."

He drinks deeply, the wine staining his lips, and sets the glass down with exaggerated grace. His eyes cut to me.

"Smile, Ellen."

I bare my teeth. It's all I can manage. The ritual continues, a grotesque pantomime of family life. He carves meat, lays slices onto plates none of us touch. He speaks of purity, of legacy, of devotion, his words laced with fervor that trembles on the edge of madness. When Sophie sobs loudly, he slams his palm on the table, the cutlery rattling.

"Silence."

She goes still, hiccupping, clutching Amelia's arm. I stare at the candles until their flames blur and dance. In the distorted light, I see Isobel's face. Every portrait, every brushstroke, the final canvas of her deathbed. And I know with clarity colder than snow that he is trying to breathe her back into life through us.

The meal ends not with thanks but with silence, the air thick with smoke and dread. He rises, adjusts his cuffs, and gestures toward me.

"Come."

I rise, legs shaking, and he escorts me back toward the Blue Suite. The girls trail behind Mrs. Lennox, their small figures swallowed by shadow. At the door, he presses a kiss to my forehead, his lips cold despite the heat.

"Perfect," he whispers. "You are perfect."

Then he leaves me in the room with the lilies on the wallpaper and the ghost of Isobel's perfume.

Alone in the Blue Suite, my body trembles in the violet gown, the silk clinging damp to my skin. My reflection in the mirror looks like a stranger, a pale imitation of a woman long dead.

I sink onto the edge of the bed, my hands pressed to my face. I can still hear Sophie's sobs, Amelia's defiance, Stuart's voice raised in grotesque prayer. The lodge hums around me, its silence pressing, its walls swollen with secrets. No more.

I cross to the dressing table. On its surface sits a silver-backed brush, a jar of powder, a shallow dish scattered with trinkets. Among them lies an ornate hairpin, long and slender, tipped with a small pearl. I lift it carefully, testing its strength. The metal is sturdy, the tip narrow. It could easily be coaxed into a lock. My hands shake as I slip it into the sleeve of the gown. I whisper to my reflection in the mirror, to the hollow-eyed woman who has watched me vanish piece by piece.

"No more waiting. Tomorrow, we leave."

The words taste foreign, dangerous, but also clean. I sit back on the bed, the pin hidden against my skin, the diary under my pillow, Moira's letter tucked in the mattress. Pieces of defiance, small but real.

My hands tremble, but my mind is set. If I fail, he will destroy us all. If I succeed, we might just live. I close my eyes and whisper one final vow into the silence. "For Amelia. For Sophie. For me."

Tomorrow, the noose tightens, or it breaks and we fall.

22

The Blue Suite is awash in cold light. I lie still, listening to Stuart's movements in the study below, faint as a tide through floorboards. I can hear him settle in his chair, and shortly afterwards, I hear the unmistakable rumble of his snoring. I take it as my cue.

The hairpin is hidden in the pocket of my gown. My fingers are stiff from the cold, but they know what to do. I slip from the bed, wrap myself in a shawl, and move like a shadow up the service stair towards the attic. Each step protests, wood creaking at my weight, but he won't hear it from his study. My heart thunders against my ribs as if it wants out.

The attic door is ahead, hunched at the end of a narrow corridor that smells of dust and old paint. The lock is rust-stiff, but the hairpin finds its throat. I coax, I breathe, and I pray. A click, so small it might be the house shifting. Then the door yields.

Inside, the air is thin, the cold gnawing. Moonlight seeps through gaps in the shutters, silvering the rafters. And there, my girls, Amelia and Sophie, huddle under a single moth-eaten blanket, eyes wide. They scramble to me, clutching at my gown, even as I warn them to stay quiet as mice.

"Mom," Sophie whispers, voice small, a whimper wrapped in the word.

I gather them close, breathing in their warmth. My throat burns with relief, but there's no time for tears. "Shh. We don't have long. Listen."

I crouch low, my arms around them both, whispering the plan as if the shadows might steal it. "At dawn, we slip out the service entrance. The big door he doesn't watch. We'll cross the lake. It's frozen thick. Once we reach the road, someone will come by. We'll wave them down. We'll be free."

Sophie clutches her doll so tightly the button eye digs into her palm. "The lake?" Her lips tremble. "What if it breaks?"

"It won't," I lie, my voice steady even as my gut knots. "I checked the window. The ice is strong. We'll make it."

Amelia lifts her chin, eyes fierce. "We can be brave, Mom. I can help with Sophie." She squeezes her sister's shoulder. "I'll hold her hand."

The weight of their trust presses harder than the lodge's walls. One misstep, one sound, one crack in the ice, and I'll lose them both. I smooth Sophie's hair, kiss Amelia's temple.

"At first light," I whisper. "Be ready. Don't make a sound. Not one."

They nod, small solemn warriors. For a moment we just hold each other, three beating hearts in a room that reeks of ghosts. I tuck the blanket tighter around them and steal one last look at their faces. Amelia's steady, Sophie's trembling, both of them unmistakably mine. Then I slip back through the door, closing it softly, heart hammering at the thought of what's to come.

The service stair is cold and narrow, the kind of passage made for servants who were never meant to be heard. My shawl snags on a nail and nearly tears. I freeze, breath caught.

Then I hear a creak that doesn't belong to me. I turn, and my blood runs cold. Stuart stands at the bottom of the stair, a shadow among shadows. The moonlight catches his eyes, making them gleam like an animal's in the dark. His posture is relaxed, but the silence around him is a trap closing.

"You shouldn't be wandering, my darling." His voice is low, soft, but it carries the weight of iron.

My hands tremble, hidden in my shawl.

"I couldn't sleep," I whisper. "The night has me restless."

He ascends a step, then another, moving slowly, deliberately. His hand finds my elbow, guiding me down. Seemingly gentle, but his grip is steel disguised in velvet. The stairwell closes around us. His body heat presses at my side.

"The night is no place for you to wander," he murmurs, fingers tightening just enough to remind me of my place. "You don't want to wake the children."

Each step toward the Blue Suite feels like a descent into the grave. My skin crawls, and every nerve shrieks with the question. Did he see me? Did he hear? Back in the room, he lingers for a moment. His hand slides from my elbow to my shoulder, then lifts to stroke my hair.

"You belong here," he says softly, almost tender. "Don't forget that."

He leaves me trembling, closing the door behind him. But in the silence that follows, I can't shake the feeling that Stuart already knows my plan. That he has always known. And that he is waiting.

23

Dawn arrives like a blade, thin, sharp, and without apology. Even the lodge lies still, as if it has understood there is a line between night and morning and we are about to step over it.

I wake the girls in a whisper, touching each of their shoulders the way you touch a sleeping bird, with just enough pressure to rouse them, but not enough to frighten. Amelia opens her eyes at once, already braced, the way a soldier might be in a trench with the sun not yet up. Sophie's lashes flutter, and she makes the small kitten-sound she makes when she doesn't want to leave a warm dream.

"It's time," I murmur. "Shoes. Coats. Quiet as the snow."

Amelia nods and slides from the bed without a squeak. She helps Sophie into her boots, her clumsy fingers tugging laces with more urgency than skill. I fold scarves around their small necks, wrap mittens over their even smaller hands. When I open the door, the corridor lies empty and pale, a rib cage of shadows and paneling.

We take the service stair that curls downward like a secret thought. The boards complain faintly, and I flinch at each noise, then force my shoulders to loosen so the creaks don't multiply.

Amelia holds Sophie's hand. Sophie holds her doll. I hold the hairpin hidden in my sleeve like a sword, as if its small strip of metal could protect us from everything that lives in these walls.

At the mudroom, the smell of cold sneaks under the door, the breath of snow. I lift the latch. It sounds so loud I think it will wake the house, rouse the portraits, alert the men who hang inside them. The door opens onto a yard molded into white humps and hollows, where the snow drifts look like the backs of sleeping animals. Wind moves across the yard in low, steady lines, combing ripples into the powder. We step into the morning.

Our boots punch holes in the snow's crust. The cold is a hand that presses the air thin, presses it straight through my clothes and into the soft parts under my ribs. The service path shows itself in gray humps, where men have shoveled and the snow has disobeyed by falling back again. The forest stands beyond, black and bristled, hemming the lodge on three sides the way a crowd hems a cage.

We go. One foot, then the other. Breath in short white stitches. The sound of snow underfoot is shockingly loud, like tiny detonations, each crunch the size of our whole lives. We keep to the path until the trees take us in. Their limbs bend low with their burden, the branches murmuring as they shed small cascades of sugar snow that pat-pat onto our shoulders and heads.

"Almost there," I whisper, though the truth is we have a mile of woods before the lake. "Quiet as mice."

Amelia squeezes Sophie's hand.

"Quiet as foxes," she corrects softly, because foxes know how to live even when the world doesn't want them to.

We slip into the trees. The forest swallows the lodge behind us and the house shrinks to an idea, then to a superstition. Snow sculpts everything into gentler shapes out here. Rocks become loaves, fallen branches make sleeping limbs, tree roots are the backs of whales. Our passage is a stuttering seam across all that smoothness. Boot, boot, boot. Breath, breath, breath.

I choose the route I walked in my head all night, following the game trail that skirts the hill, the older logging road buried under drift, the low line between the birches where the ground doesn't pitch. The lake is due east. The road is further east of that. Run straight and you will find a mercy. Run crooked and you will circle back to the door you tried to leave by.

A clink lands in the air far behind us. A torch, kissed by a ring on a man's hand. Every part of me goes cold in a new way that has nothing to do with the snow and everything to do with terror.

"Faster," I whisper, and our three gaits catch a new rhythm. Sophie stumbles. Amelia rights her with a swift tug and a whispered, "You're doing it. You're doing it."

The sound comes again, followed by the dull stomp of boots tamping crust. I don't look back. Looking back is the luxury of people who are not prey.

"Ellen."

My name in that voice travels through the trees like a thrown rope.

"Where are you going?"

His question is polite, almost amused, as if he has caught me stealing my own coat and would like a joke to go with it. I don't turn. If I see his face, I will remember the version of him that can be gentled by a kiss, and I will die where I stand.

Branches whip my shoulders, my hips. The forest is a tangle of hands. The snow snatches at our ankles, and drags like a mouth. Amelia takes the brunt of it for Sophie, cutting a path, her knees high, her breaths fierce. She keeps her head up. She never looks back either.

"Ellen!" The voice sounds closer now, without the cushion of the house to soften it. "Don't do this. Come back. The girls are cold. You're frightened. This is madness."

Torchlight gathers and looses itself among the trunks behind us, swinging, pooling, and vanishing. It becomes a fourth thing in the forest, besides the trees, besides us, that knows where it is going. When he speaks again, the warmth is gone and the threat is full.

"You belong with me."

We break the game trail where it folds under a fallen pine. I throw my weight against the snow-buried trunk and heave it aside just enough for the girls to squeeze through. Snow buries itself down the collars of our coats, cold coins on hot skin. Sophie squeaks and Amelia claps a mitten to her mouth, gentler than a gag, the gesture an apology.

"Nearly there," I lie through my teeth. "We'll see the lake in a minute."

The ground tips down. It would be easy to fall, easier to slide, but sliding makes noise you can't control, so we step, small and brutal, stamping footholds into the slope. Above us, a crow complains once, then loses interest. The world is too white for its black to matter.

A new sound breaks the air. The dry crrrK of ice settling deep under layers of snow. The lake is close enough to speak to us. Hope rises so fast I almost trip on it.

"Don't run from me!" He's angry now, the silk gone from his voice. "Don't embarrass yourself. Don't embarrass them."

We crest the last rise. The trees loosen and fling us toward a white so open it feels like standing on the roof of the sky. The lake lies ahead, a sheet of pewter buried under frost, its edge scalloped where snow has been pushed by wind into curled lips. The far bank is a black line. Beyond that, the road is out there somewhere. Waiting to carry us home. I tell myself that until it feels more true than the man in the trees.

The shore ice is ribbed and mean, a churn of frozen waves and broken water turned to glass and trapped in the act. Someone with sense would walk the shore to the point and cross where the lake pinches. But someone with sense is not being hunted by a man who uses portraits instead of bars.

"Mom," Amelia hisses. "We have to go. Now."

We go. The first step onto the lake is like stepping onto a giant treacherous cloud. The ice gives, a fraction, the snow whispering, the cold pushing back. A half-crack speaks under my right boot, just a small one, but the sound is like knuckles. It echoes outward across the sheet and returns to us magnified, ricocheting off the far bank. Sophie jerks. Amelia squeezes her hand so tight their mittens squeal.

"Quiet feet," I whisper. "Flat feet. Spread the weight. Just like I told you."

We haven't practiced anything but being taught to obey, then teaching ourselves to disobey as quietly as possible. We move into the white. The wind comes for us with teeth, now that the trees don't blunt it. It finds every seam in our coats. It takes the air right out of our mouths and spits it back in our faces as flecks of ice. The girls' breath makes two little steam engines. Mine is a saw, push, pull, push, pull, on a log that will not give.

We get ten paces. Twenty. The lake speaks from deep in its belly. It sounds like a mythical whale that remembers being a mountain. The sound walks up the bones in my calves, lodges behind my teeth, hums there like fear.

"That's it," Amelia whispers to Sophie, an adult's steadiness in a child's pitch. "Think about cake. Think of all the lovely cake."

Sophie nods miserably and tries not to cry. Tears would freeze. I tell myself this is a mercy. That the cold is keeping us from the hot, salt-wet panic that would take our feet out from under us. I tell myself a lot of things trying to make my body believe just one of them. We reach the middle of the lake precisely the way you reach the end of a life you didn't choose, by taking the next step because it is the only step.

"Where are you going?"

The voice slices the white.

Still, I cannot not turn. I risk a glance over my shoulder, just to see how far he is from us. To check if we can make it. Stuart stands on the far bank, the torch dark now, dangling from his fingers. Fury has stripped him to principle. In that moment he is not a man but a rule. One that says you will not leave.

I pull the girls closer, and hurry them on, my hands digging into their coats.

"Don't look," I say, though I have looked for him, to measure the yards between him and us, the yards between us and mercy. "Just keep walking, quickly."

He steps forward onto the ice. It groans under him as if a god has put a foot onto the belly of a sleeping animal. He does not test it with a stick, does not kneel to spread his weight, none of the things a man raised by winter would do. He simply believes the lake will hold him because everything here has always held him. He was born and the house became a heart. He speaks and rooms obey. Why wouldn't the lake be obedient too? He walks. We walk faster.

"Ellen," he calls, calmer again now, the priest returned to the pulpit. "You don't know what you're doing."

He seems to cover distance the way a man does who has never been told no twice in the same moment. The cracks flit from beneath his boots in delicate tracery, then heal, then flit again faster. The ice under my own feet registers his weight as a rumor, tick, tick, then as a confession, crrrK, then as a threat that makes my kneecaps burn.

Sophie falters. Not a stumble, exactly, more the full-body flinch of a small person whose nervous system has decided to save itself by laying down. She sinks to her knees, mittens skidding.

"I can't," she whispers, and the words make me blind.

"You can," Amelia says, her voice a wire that holds. She hauls Sophie up by the armpits with the ugly, efficient strength of a child who has done so much lifting already. "You're doing it. We're doing it. Look at me, Soph. Not at him. Not at the ground. Look at me."

Sophie's eyes lock onto Amelia's. The wind runs at us and through us and away. We take three more steps like that, one girl pulling, the other held, me pushing them forward with my hands at their backs, as if I can deliver them to the far shore by will alone.

"Where are you going, Ellen?" he asks again, not shouting this time. The question carries the smile of a man who could laugh if he wanted to and has chosen not to because the joke is not yet fully ripened. "What is on the other side that I cannot give you?"

A road, I think. A churchyard and a kitchen and a woman with a letter in her hand. A sheriff with a gun. A life that is not arranged like a deathbed and called a shrine. "Everything," I want to say, and instead I say nothing, because sound breaks ice. Because reason doesn't cross lakes, feet do.

A crack opens to my left like a mouth. It is not much, just a slit in the snow-fluffed surface through which a line of black water shows its teeth. My brain, traitor that it is, tells me exactly what the temperature of that water would be. It tells me exactly how long a person can remain conscious in it, and how the muscles of the chest lock first, then the hands, then the jaw.

"Mom." Amelia's voice is a needle that threads me back through the fabric of my panic. "Right. Go right."

We angle off to the right, away from the crack. The shift asks the ice a question. It answers with a long nnnooo dragged up from under the shore and sent across the skin of the lake.

Stuart sounds nearer now, close enough that I can hear the breath puffing from his mouth in precise, possessive clouds. When I glance back, there is pleasure in his face. Not the gross, grinning kind but the pleasure of a predator hunting prey he knows he will inevitably consume.

"Come back," he says. No thunder in it. No bile. Just the same tone he used the first time he asked me to sit for a painting. I've made the room warm for you. I've lit the good lamps. I've put the chair where you will look best. The voice he used that first night in the Boston Athenaeum when he told me I had seen his painting honestly. The voice he used at the wedding when he promised to keep me. He means it. That is the most dangerous part. Monsters who mean it are the kind you marry by mistake. We keep moving as fast as we can. The far bank is not so far now.

"Count," Amelia says to Sophie between her teeth, and Sophie nods, tears freezing into stars at the corners of her eyes. "One. Two. Three," they say, first together, then out of step, which means they're alive. Counting is not something dead girls do.

The ice sings under us, high, then low, then high again. Like a cathedral's organ played by weather. A huge cracking sound sees a skitter of fissures fly out from under Stuart's boot at the next step, veining toward us, prettily at first, then ragged, then fast. The lines reach for my toes and stop a foot short, like lightning reconsidering a strike. He pauses. The pause is not fear, but it is calculation. He shifts his weight and the singing changes key.

"Where are you going?" he asks again, and then softer. "I won't let you ruin what we are."

The wind takes the words and tears them like paper. I let the tearing happen. I fill the space his voice leaves with one of my own, the voice reserved for very small babies and very large dogs, steady with no room for dissent.

"Three more steps," I tell the girls. "Then three more. Then three more."

A shape moves on the shoreline ahead, and two crows lift from a scrub pine, the gray flank of a snowbank slumping a little as if relieved of its own weight. I pick a place on the bank, a darker patch where wind has combed the snow away from a tangle of roots, and appoint it salvation. If I can get their boots on that color, I will let my legs do whatever they like after.

We cross one more seam in the ice, that splits into a shallow, sugared fracture like a wrinkle on a giant's skin, and the far shore tilts toward us as if it has been leaning our way the whole time. I feel the ground under the ice rise, feel the old shore stones stacked under frozen water, the way the texture changes from long, slick strokes to short, hard ridges. We are five yards away. Four.

"Stop."

The word cracks against my spine. He has stopped. He has warned the lake with his voice, when he meant to warn me with it.

We do not stop.

"Ellen."

I don't turn. I don't waste the last of our luck on courtesy.

"Ellen," he says again, and for the first time since I have known him, there is a sound inside my name that is not command and not desire. It is the one we all live with and pretend not to hear. It is fear. His, not mine.

We step onto the shore where ice meets earth. The ice complains one last time, petulant now, like a child told to do a thing it does not want to do. Then our boots find the scruffy, wind-eaten shoulder of the bank. The difference is so small my brain refuses it. Then my knees notice. Then my lungs. Then I do.

"Good," Amelia whispers, the strongest word I have ever heard in a child's mouth.

We scramble, bodies suddenly heavy the way bodies always are once they are allowed to live. I shove the girls up the little slope with both hands. Their boots dig into old snow that has re-frozen enough times to be almost stairs. The scrub pine gives my glove a green smear. I hear the small frantic gulping noises I make when I am crying and trying not to. I do not remember crying. I only remember the sound it makes when a person is allowed to breathe again.

On the lake, he keeps coming. He is two-thirds across now, a black cutout against the white, his long coat snapping in the wind. His anger is making him careless, it makes his steps heavier, less carefully judged. The cracks around his boots lace and unlace like stitches. With each step, the lake sings higher, closer to breaking point.

We pause for a second in the lee of a drift big enough to hide us from his sight. The world here smells like pine pitch and clean cold. Amelia presses Sophie's head into her shoulder, shushing her, not because crying is bad but because sound makes maps for men.

"Listen to me." I take their faces in my hands, one on either side. "We keep going to those trees," I whisper. "Then we don't stop until the road. Do not look back. Whatever you hear, you do not look back."

"What if…" Sophie begins, and I take her mittened hand and press it to my heart, thudding under my coat.

"You keep your feet on the ground," I say. "That is all. That is everything. Do you hear me?"

They nod their jerky little yeses that mean we will try. It is the only covenant worth anything. We move on, three figures in a world that doesn't care whether we stand or fall. We run for the trees in short, ugly strides, keeping our centers low so the wind can't slow us down. The first line of trunks meets us like a crowd that is on our side. The branches take the worst of the weather and bend it another way. The needles make a sound like whispering math.

At the screech of my name again, I do what I told them not to. I look.

He is heading to where we chose the bank. He does not run. He does not need to. His progress seems inevitable, step, crack, step, crack, as if he has always been walking across every lake that ever froze just for him. He lifts his face. For a breath, in that blank light, he is beautiful the way statues are, perfection poured over a thing until its errors cannot breathe. He looks like a man who has never learned the word no and believes it is a profanity when spoken by someone other than himself. He looks like the last thing a deer sees.

I turn back into the trees because I cannot bear to grant him the dignity of being the last thing I see. We run. The snow in the forest is deeper than on the lake. It's a slowed world. A world that makes you pay for your forward motion in coins of breath. We push through it.

Behind us, the ice sings higher. A sound like a string snapping on a violin carries out across the white. Another, lower, and meaner, full of weight. The lake is talking to itself about the line between holding and letting go.

"Don't look," I tell the girls, and I don't either. But the sound that comes next is not one a human being can ignore. It is bigger than us, older than timber and vow. It is the sound a thing makes when it decides it will no longer obey. A crack like thunder splits the air, followed by a guttural scream.

We don't stop. We can't. But I turn just before the trees swallow us, and I see him fall through the ice into the icy black of the lake. I see his face turn from anger to disbelief to shock.

"Don't look!" I shout again, more to myself than the girls. I grab bark with one hand, drag myself up a small rise, push the girls ahead. Amelia reaches back for me and I push her hand away and push her forward.

"Go."

We go. And, when I glance back again, he is gone. And just a black hole gapes in the ice like a mouth that's finally consumed its last meal.

I turn, and run after the girls, not waiting to confirm his fate. Stuart is not a man to go lightly. The forest takes us deeper in, the ground rising where it should, dipping where it must. I keep the lake on our left, the idea of the road in my head like a star you can't see but know exists. The wind threads its way through the trunks and loses its temper, reduced to a hiss. Our breaths become the loudest thing again. That is how you know you are not prey anymore, when your own body sounds like the biggest animal.

When at last we stop, it's only because Sophie's legs shake so hard they threaten to give out. The lake is only a dull silver through the trees now. The far bank we left is a smear. The lodge is a story. My heart is a drum that will not admit there are other instruments.

Amelia presses her ear to Sophie's hat. "You're okay," she tells her, and even if it is a lie it is the most useful one we have.

"Keep going," I say, because saying it will keep us honest, and because the only truth that has ever saved me is the one with feet in it.

We start again, and this time I don't look back at all. Not because I am brave. Because I am finished with the sight of him. Because the only direction that contains a life is the direction in which his name is not a god.

We move toward the road, toward the village. When the first line of birches thins and the trees give us a slit of sky, the wind changes. It brings a smell no forest ever made. It's soft, human, and hopeful. Smoke from a chimney, a waft of baking bread. It folds itself into our lungs and warms us on.

"Almost," I whisper, and this time it isn't a lie, and this time no voice answers from behind asking where we are going.

And then I see the road. At first, it's just a cut through the trees, darker, broader than its surroundings. A flat stretch lined with snow-buried fences. But it's a road with tire tracks softened by the night's storm, and it promises other people exist beyond the suffocating forest.

My knees buckle. I half-carry, half-drag the girls onto the packed snow of the road. The relief is so violent I could weep. But there's no time. The wind changes, bringing with it not just the clean sting of pine, but the faintest murmur of voices.

"Hello?" My voice breaks, raw from cold and fear. "Help us! Please!"

At first, I think I've conjured them, those figures moving through the trees ahead in dark coats against the pale snow. But then the shapes grow clearer. Two men in heavy wool, rifles slung on their backs, breath misting. And between them, steady, determined, her scarf whipped around her face by the wind, is Moira O'Donnell.

"God above," she breathes when she sees us. She runs the last few paces. "Ellen."

Her arms fold around me before I can collapse, but collapse I do, into her shoulder, into warmth, into the scent of smoke and soap instead of perfume and rot. My body gives up its weight, surrendering the fight to someone else at last.

"It's over," I whisper into her coat, words blurred with tears. "It's over."

Behind me, Amelia clings to Sophie, who sobs against her

sister's chest. Amelia meets Moira's eyes over Sophie's shoulder, her face pale and young again. Moira pulls back just enough to look at me. Her eyes are dark, steady.

"No, love," she says softly, firmly. "You're safe now, but with men like him..." She glances back toward the lake, toward the white expanse stretching silent behind the trees. "It's not over until he's gone."

The words hollow me out. Relief floods me, but dread sits right beside it, a twin in the same body. Because she's right. Lakes close over secrets. And houses like Drummond Lodge were built to keep them.

The men speak low to each other, one shrugging off his coat to drape over Amelia and Sophie, the other steadying me by the arm.

"Let's get them to town," one mutters. "The sheriff will want to hear everything."

Moira doesn't take her eyes off me.

"You've done the hardest part," she whispers, squeezing my hand, pressing her strength into my bones. "Now we'll keep you safe."

But even as I nod, even as I let them guide us down the road toward smoke and roofs and people, the cold thought remains. Stuart is gone, or so the ice told us, but I didn't actually see him swallowed up. Just the absence of him where he had been. And I know with a terrible certainty that escaping his house is not the same as escaping him. Not yet, anyway.

24

The town looks like another world without Mrs Lennox guiding my every move through it. The main street is lined with squat brick buildings shouldering each other against the wind, their windows glowing faintly behind frost. Smoke threads from chimneys into the pale morning. It smells of bacon grease and wood ash, and promises safety.

The sheriff's office sits between a diner and the post office, its door heavy oak worn smooth by years of palms. The sign above is faded, letters chipped. Adirondack County Sheriff. Moira holds it open for me as if she knows my hands are too raw and bloodied to manage it. Sophie clings to my side, Amelia steadying her with one hand.

Inside, the warmth from a potbelly stove makes my bones ache with sudden thaw. Antlers crown the wall above a cluttered desk. Maps of the county fan across corkboards, the lake a frozen gray smear cutting through them. Sheriff O'Donnell stands behind the desk. He is a heavy man with broad shoulders and a trimmed mustache gone mostly gray. His presence fills the room the way authority fills silence, thick and demanding attention. His eyes flick from me, to the girls, then to Moira.

"Christ," he mutters, soft but sharp, pulling a chair forward. "Sit her down."

I don't argue. The wood bites cold through my coat, but the solid feel steadies me. Sophie slides onto my lap, curling against me like she used to when she was a baby. Amelia takes the other chair Moira offers and perches straight-backed, as if she means to prove her worth in this room. Moira keeps a hand on my shoulder, her strength a lifeline.

"They made it out across the ice," she tells her husband. "Stuart Drummond chased them."

His brows lift, disbelief flickering. "Chased them?"

I open my mouth before she can soften it.

"He hunted us," I whisper. "Like prey."

The sheriff's gaze settles on me, weighing. "Start from the beginning, Mrs. Drummond. What happened in that house?"

I take a shuddering breath. The words taste heavy, dangerous, but once I let them out, they can't be taken back. "He locked me away. He dressed me in his mother's clothes, put me in her room, the Blue Suite. He said I was her. That I belonged to him the way she had."

Sophie squirms, whimpering softly. I stroke her hair, forcing my voice steady.

"There was a diary. It was Isobel's. She wrote about how he, or his father, watched her, and controlled her, how she was fading. Stuart worshipped her for it. He painted her. Over and over. As she got sicker, thinner, weaker. He thought her dying was beautiful."

Sheriff O'Donnell shifts, his jaw tight. "Paintings?"

Amelia leans forward, her small voice firm. "We saw them in the attic. Dozens of them. She looked... like a ghost."

I swallow.

"He wanted the same for me. He said he would keep me forever. Paint me into eternity."

Moira's hand squeezes my shoulder. Her eyes are dark, steady, daring her husband to dismiss it. The sheriff exhales through his nose, leaning back in his chair.

"You're saying he meant to… what? Kill you?" the Sheriff asks.

"He doesn't see it that way." My voice rises, sharper. "To him, it's devotion. Art. He believes death is perfection. That letting Isobel waste away was making her eternal."

My hands tremble against Sophie's small frame.

"He wanted me to be his next canvas."

The room is quiet except for the stove's low hiss. The sheriff studies me, his face kind. Finally, he says, "And this morning? What happened on the ice?"

My throat tightens. Images flash of the cracks spreading, the lake roaring, the black hole in the icy crust.

"He chased us through the woods. He nearly caught us on the lake. We made it to the other side, but the ice broke under him. He went through."

The sheriff nods slowly, rubbing his mustache. "So, he's dead?"

The words clang in my skull. Dead. The word I want most. The word I can't trust. I shake my head.

"I don't know. We were running. I didn't want to stop. I think he fell in. But with him…" My voice falters. "I don't know if even the lake can hold him."

Amelia's hand finds mine.

Moira looks at her husband, eyes hard. "You'll send men to the lodge. You'll drag the lake."

He lifts his brows, clearly uncomfortable with the demand. "Moira…"

"Don't you Moira me. You know what that family's been like. What they've done." Her voice is sharper than I've heard it. "Don't play the fool, Patrick."

The sheriff leans forward, palms flat on the desk. His eyes flick between us, the fury in his wife's face and the exhaustion in mine.

"I'll send men," he says finally. "We'll sweep the lodge. We'll search the lake. We'll see if the bastard's still breathing."

Relief should flood me. It doesn't. I clutch Sophie tighter.

"What if you don't find him?"

"Bodies sink in cold water," the sheriff says, pragmatic. "They resurface in spring, if they don't snag. If he's down there, we'll know eventually."

"Eventually," I echo. The word tastes like ash. Moira crouches to meet my eyes.

"He may haunt your thoughts, Ellen, but thoughts aren't men. He's flesh, and flesh drowns, or it freezes. Hold to that."

I want to. God, I want to. But I hear him still, his voice echoing from the ice. You are mine. The sheriff pulls a notebook toward him, pen scratching. "We'll need your full statement. Everything. The diary, if it exists. The paintings. Everything."

"The locked room," I say.

Moira nods grimly. "I told you," she says to her husband. "That house keeps its dead."

The sheriff frowns but writes it down, the scratching of the pen loud in the stillness as I begin to speak, recounting detail after detail. I tell him about the Blue Suite preserved as a shrine, the perfume, the shattered bottle, the hairpin hidden in my gown. I realize that the weight has shifted inside me. Terror still grips me, but now there is the offer of release. Someone is writing it all down, and someone is listening who might do something about it.

Still, dread lingers. Because Moira is right. With men like Stuart, certainty is an illusion. And until I see his body laid out cold, until I know the lake has kept him, I will never truly believe it is over.

As I spoke, I stared at the maps tacked to the wall. So many rivers, ridges, lakes, roads. A whole county filled with lives, houses, people who woke and slept without fear. But what was out there for me? The lodge was behind me, the road ahead an unknown. My marriage to Michael had ended in fire and ash. Thomas had left me with debts and silence. Now Stuart, who had promised salvation that turned to a prison, was gone, but not gone enough.

I bent my head into my hands. I had fought so hard to keep the girls safe, to get us out, but now that we were here, out in the open, the fight was beginning to drain from me. What next? Where would we sleep tonight? Who would we become tomorrow?

"Mom?" Amelia's voice was small but steady. "What do we do now?"

The question pierced me. I wanted to give her certainty, a promise, but the words caught in my throat. "I don't know," I whispered. My eyes filled hot, blurring the antlers on the wall, the maps, the stove. "I don't know, Amelia. But whatever we do, we'll be alright. Just us, together."

Moira moved then, crossing to crouch beside me. Her hand rested warm on my knee, firm enough to tether me back to the room. Her voice was low but unyielding. "You survived. That's the first thing. Don't cheapen it by expecting answers this very moment. Survival comes first. The rest, the what you do, where you go, who you become? Well, that comes after."

Her eyes met mine, steady and unsparing. "I know you feel lost. I know fear doesn't vanish just because the door's unlocked. But hear me: you are not nothing without him. He wanted you to believe that, because it kept you still. But you proved him wrong. You moved. You got your girls across that lake."

I swallowed hard. The truth of it sat heavy in my chest.

Moira leaned closer, her voice softening. "You think you're

broken, Ellen, but broken women don't plan escapes. Broken women don't carry children through storms. You're stronger than you know. What you need now is time, and a place that doesn't speak his name."

I stared at her, words trapped under my tongue. My tears slipped hot onto my cheeks. Sophie shifted in my lap, half-asleep now, her thumb in her mouth. Amelia had turned toward us, her eyes shining but dry, her lips curling into a tight, proud, defiant smile. Moira squeezed my knee once more, then withdrew. She straightened, fussed with the stove, poured water from a kettle into chipped mugs. The steam rose between us, a curtain of something ordinary and warm.

I closed my eyes, hearing the clatter of pots beyond the walls, the murmur of townsfolk outside starting their day. Life went on, indifferent to the horrors of the lodge. And somehow, impossibly, we were still in it.

I breathed, deep and ragged, and whispered into Sophie's hair: "We're alive."

The words felt strange, new in my mouth. But real. And as I held onto them, the weight of the past didn't vanish, but it shifted, just slightly, enough to let me draw another breath.

25

The girls had dozed off on a bench near the stove, Sophie curled into Amelia's lap, their small bodies tangled together like they had shared one womb. Their cheeks were flushed from heat, boots still streaked with lake frost. I sat close enough to reach them with one hand, as if letting go for a moment might invite disaster back through the door.

The hinges groaned. Sheriff O'Donnell stepped inside, his boots wet, his hat rimmed with snowmelt. His face was harder to read than ever. Moira, perched in the chair beside me, straightened.

"Well?" she asked, her voice sharp.

The sheriff glanced at the girls before answering. Then, with a sigh that seemed to empty the room, he said: "Nothing. No body."

The words struck me like cold water. My stomach hollowed out, my pulse stuttered.

"Nothing?" My voice was thin, brittle. "But he fell through."

The sheriff rubbed a hand over his face. "Ice was fractured where you said. Big hole, frozen over already at the edges. We dragged as far as we could reach. Not a trace."

Moira's lips pressed tight. "And the house?"

The sheriff's jaw ticked. "We searched every room. The servants' quarters are stripped bare. Nobody there either. But the west wing..." He shook his head. "Dozens of canvases. Stacks of them. Portraits of his mother. Portraits of you."

My skin prickled, hot and clammy at once. "Of me?"

He nodded. "Half-finished. Same poses as hers. Same... decline. Looks like he'd already started painting you into her place. Into her death."

The room spun. For a moment, I thought I might faint. My voice came out a rasp. "So it's true. Everything I feared..."

Moira reached for my hand, her grip steady. "You knew it in your bones. Now it's written on canvas."

The sheriff cleared his throat, uncomfortable. "Some of the men wanted to torch the whole wing. But the place is stone. Wouldn't catch easy."

"Good," Moira said. "It deserves to rot. Let it fall in on itself."

But I couldn't picture rot. I could only picture the paintings, and the oils thick and glistening. My body immortalized as a corpse before I was one. His worship made permanent. My stomach heaved.

"What if he didn't drown?" The words escaped me before I could stop them. "What if he's still out there? Watching?"

The sheriff's eyes softened a fraction. "Cold like that, he'd have minutes at most. No man survives long in that water."

Moira, though, didn't soften. She leaned close, her voice low. "Minutes are enough for a man like him. Enough to crawl, to hide, to wait. Don't mistake silence for safety."

Her words should have terrified me. Instead, they anchored me in a strange way. She wasn't promising fairy tales. She was giving me the truth, bitter but useful.

The sheriff pulled off his gloves, laying them on the desk.

"For now, you're safe. Stay here tonight. Tomorrow we'll

arrange something more permanent, maybe take statements from the girls if they're up to it." He eyed Amelia and Sophie again, his face shadowed with something like pity. "They're brave. Braver than most grown men I know."

I brushed a curl of hair from Amelia's forehead. She stirred but didn't wake. Brave. The word sat heavy on me. I didn't want them brave. I wanted them children again. When the sheriff stepped outside to join his men, the office felt smaller still, just the four of us and the stove hissing. Moira studied me, her head tilted.

"You're thinking of him," she said. Not a question.

I nodded, helpless. "Even if the lake took him, he's still here." I tapped my temple. "In here. His voice. His hands. The way he made me believe I was nothing without him."

Moira's face softened, though her eyes stayed hard. "That's the last lie he ever told you. You brought your girls across the ice, Ellen. You faced him. You survived. That is not nothing. That is everything."

Her words landed, slow as stones into deep water. Rippling. I wanted to believe them. I looked at the girls again. Sophie had her thumb back in her mouth. Amelia's arm curled around her, protective, even in sleep. My heart fractured with pride and grief.

"What do I do now?" I whispered.

"You live," Moira said simply. "You live until fear loosens its grip. You feed your girls. You make small choices, and they add up. One day you'll wake and realize he hasn't followed you into the morning. Not anymore."

Her words were steady, iron forged in the shape of kindness. I clung to them, even as dread coiled in my chest. Because she was right, there was no certainty. Stuart's body hadn't been found. His house still stood. His obsession was painted onto canvases that once held breath and skin. Relief and dread lived side by side in me, twinned. We had escaped, but not cleanly. The lodge, the ice, his voice would always cling.

Moira shifted her chair closer and took my hands in hers. Her palms were warm, work-rough, real.

"Listen to me," she said, voice low enough not to wake the girls. "Water like that is a killer. Patrick's pulled more than a few from the lakes up here. Snowmobilers, ice-fishermen who thought the black spots would hold, drunks who misjudged the shoreline at night. In water that cold, a man has minutes. Not even that, sometimes. The blood leaves the limbs first, runs to save the heart. The muscles seize. The breath locks. It's not will, it's the body saying no."

I tried to picture Stuart arguing with his own heart and losing. My breath stuttered.

Moira squeezed once, hard.

"He didn't survive it, Ellen. He can't have. But winter is a lid. That lake keeps what it takes until spring. When the thaw comes, the ice pulls back from the coves and the water warms just enough that everything it kept rises. Patrick hates those weeks, but he knows them. He'll put a watch on the inlets when the melt starts. If the lake has him, it'll give him up then."

"Spring," I echoed. It sounded like a date set for execution and it sounded like mercy delayed. "How long until then?"

"Depends on the year," she said. "April, sometimes May." A shadow of a smile ghosted her mouth. "Up here, spring is rude. It barges in without knocking, and the mud tells you before the flowers do."

The practical certainty in her soothed something raw. "And if... if he snagged under the ice..."

"Then it might be longer," she said, not flinching. "But bodies don't keep secrets well. Gases build. Fish talk. The lake tells in its own time." She tipped her head toward the door through which the sheriff had gone. “And Patrick knows how to listen.”

The image came unbidden of green water dark as tea, a coat tangling on drowned branches, a face turned pale and empty to an underside of ice. I shut my eyes against it and felt Sophie’s small weight settle harder into my lap, her breath gone soft and whistling with sleep.

“I can’t keep them braced for months,” I whispered. “I can’t keep waking every night to listen for him.”

“You won’t,” Moira said. “Not every night. Maybe the first many. Fewer after. Fear’s a tide. It’s high at first, then it learns to ebb if you let it.” She released one of my hands to brush a curl off Amelia’s brow.

“Spring,” I said again, tasting it. “We wait for spring.”

“And we don’t do it alone,” Moira said, as if spring were a creature that spooked easily and needed coaxing.

The sheriff cleared his throat as he came back in. He glanced at Amelia and Sophie. “I’ll need to ask the older one a few questions when she wakes,” he said gently. “Not now. Later. We’ll go careful. No pictures,” he added quickly, as if reading my mind about the hungry press. “No gawkers in this office. I’ll send them packing.”

Moira’s mouth turned satisfied again. “You see why I married him,” she murmured to me, and for a heartbeat something like lightness visited and passed.

The heat drowsed me. My head nodded, jerked, nodded again. Every time my eyes closed, I saw a black mouth open in white, saw a coat vanish. I forced them open to find the room unchanged, with the antlers still above, the maps still pinned, the girls still breathing where their bodies lay in a knot.

“What if spring comes and there’s still… nothing?” I asked, surprised to hear the question out loud. “What if the lake keeps him the way the lodge kept everything else? What if he chooses to haunt instead of rise?"

Moira laid her hand over mine again. "Then we make a grave anyway," she said. "People do it for wars all the time. For ships. They stand on dirt and bury air and say the words that let their lives proceed. The body isn't the permission, Ellen. The choosing is."

The sheriff nodded, reluctant and sincere.

"We'll file what we need to file either way. A man can be dead for the purposes that matter to the living without a coroner saying so. Your safety isn't a lake's timetable."

The idea felt like a door cracking open somewhere I hadn't known there was a wall.

"A grave without a body," I said. "An end without the proof I want."

"It's not the proof that frees you," Moira said. "It's the ending."

Silence settled again, but it was the kind that comes after the worst has been named and nothing in the room has broken. Outside, a plow passed with a low, consoling roar. The window glass hummed.

26

Boston in March is a different creature from the mountains. The air smells of salt and thawing pavement, not pine and snow. Pigeons wheel above the Common, buses roar past with wet streaks down their sides, and the sidewalks are slush at noon and ice again by dusk. But it is alive. The city hums, always. You can feel it in your chest, in the soles of your feet.

Our new apartment sits on the third floor of a brick building just off Tremont Street. Two bedrooms, a kitchen with old tiles that don't match, and windows that rattle when the trolleys go by. To me it is palatial. To Amelia and Sophie, it is an adventure, stairs to climb, neighbors to spy on, a roof that sheds snow in thunderous sheets they cheer at like fireworks. And freedom from rules.

I've been here three months. Three months since the lake, since Moira, since the lodge. I haven't spoken Stuart's name aloud in that time, and yet he lives in my head like a tenant who refuses to move out. Still, life has begun to take shape around him, pressing his shadow thinner.

I found work that was steadier than I dared hope. A magazine on Boylston, glossy covers, headlines about politics, fashion, city living. They needed someone for copy, a stringer who could turn out articles on short deadlines. I've written about everything from new restaurants to a profile on a woman who keeps bees on her Cambridge rooftop. Words come easier now than sleep, but they pay, and they keep me anchored and distracted.

The girls are thriving. Sophie has a best friend in the building, a dark-eyed little boy who shares his Lego and once gave her a paper crown he'd cut out himself. Amelia reads library books as if they're fuel, her nose always pressed deep, her lips moving silently. She smiles more now, though her eyes still track every shadow in a room before she settles.

This morning, they are wild with excitement. It's St. Patrick's Day, and Boston is a sea of green. Parades, floats, bagpipes, streets lined with shamrocks. Sophie is already dressed in a bright jumper with a sequined clover on the front. Amelia wears a green scarf and pretends she is too old for such things, though she smiled when I braided her hair and pinned it with a ribbon.

I sit at the table sipping coffee that tastes faintly of burnt toast, watching them whirl around the room. My heart is tight with gratitude and terror both. To be here. To have them safe. To know the world can still hold parades after everything.

The phone rings. It's an old sound, but its shrill cry cuts the room. Sophie freezes mid-spin, then runs to grab it.

"Mom! The phone!"

I rise, already uneasy. Few people have this number. I take the receiver.

"Hello?"

"Ellen."

Her voice is unmistakable. Moira. Warm, firm, threaded with iron. The sound of it floods me with memories of her hand on my knee in the sheriff's office, and her words. Spring will give him up.

I press the receiver harder to my ear.

"Moira. Is everything all right?"

A pause. On her end, I hear wind, the creak of wood. Then her voice, low.

"They've dragged the lake. Every cove, every inlet, every tangle of root. They've searched from dawn until dark for days. They found timbers, nets, an old sled sunk in the shallows. But Ellen... no body. Not a bone. Not a shred of cloth."

My knees weaken. I grip the counter for balance.

"What are you saying?"

"I'm saying what I didn't want to say until I was sure." Moira's voice tightens. "He's not there. He's not anywhere."

The words ring through me like the toll of a bell. My breath stumbles.

"But... he went under. The ice broke."

"I know what you saw. I know what should have been." She exhales, long, sharp. "But lakes don't lie. If he'd drowned, he'd be ours by now. He isn't."

The kitchen tilts. I press my hand flat to the wall, eyes closed, stomach hollow. Stuart is alive. Out there somewhere.

"Patrick says we'll keep looking," Moira continues, softer.

The girls are watching me. Sophie with wide, uncertain eyes. Amelia with a frown, reading me as she always does, already suspicious. Moira's voice drops to almost a whisper.

"Be ready. If he's out there, he will come for what he thinks is his."

I can't breathe. My chest constricts, every sound in the room muffled, as if I'm under ice myself.

"I have to go," Moira says quickly. "Patrick's calling. But remember, don't let the quiet fool you. Promise me."

"I promise," I whisper, though my lips barely shape the words.

The line goes dead. For a moment I stand frozen, the receiver still pressed to my ear, the cord taut. Then, slowly, I lower it back onto the hook. My hand trembles. Sophie pads closer, clutching her doll.

"Mommy? Who was it?"

I force a smile. "Just a friend." My voice cracks. Amelia steps forward, her eyes narrowed, searching my face. She sees so much. Always has.

"What's wrong?"

The truth lodges in my throat. I want to tell them everything. I want to say that the lake gave nothing back, that the man who haunted us is still breathing air somewhere. But their faces are bright with anticipation, their cheeks pink, they have ribbons in their hair. They were about to walk out into streets full of music and joy. I swallow hard. My voice comes out quiet, final.

"I'm not feeling well."

Amelia tilts her head. Sophie frowns.

"We'll stay in today," I say, forcing steadiness. "No parade. Just us. Here."

Sophie's lip trembles. "But—"

"Tomorrow," I say quickly. "We'll do something tomorrow."

They nod reluctantly. Amelia studies me a moment longer, then leads Sophie back to the couch, pulling her close. I turn to the window. Outside, the street bustles with green hats, flags, laughter. The world is celebrating. And inside me, a pit opens, deep and cold. Because Moira is right. If he's alive, he's still out there, and he is waiting.

EPILOGUE

The world believes lakes are graves. They are not. They are wombs. Cold, dark, and serviceable. They keep what matters until it is ready to return in a better shape.

I sit in the quiet of my rooms, three floors up over a street that hums like a low, contented animal. The city furnishes percussion. My paint fumes make a thin skin on the air. I have always liked that sting at the back of the throat, it smells like a promise. The canvas on the easel is still wet where I want it wet, drying where I want it faithful. A portrait becomes obedient by degrees. It is Ellen.

She is not easy to catch. Isobel was easy. Her body cooperated with instruction, like a good instrument. But Ellen resists. Resistance is a better muse than compliance. There is more light to bend, more shadow to coax into the proper submission. Her mouth refuses sentimental shapes. Good. Sentiment is for amateurs and policemen.

I add a filament of pale along the cheekbone, the one that lifts when she pretends to be fine. I stop, step back. No. There's too much charity in that stroke. I wipe it away with my thumb, leave a thin bruise of color instead. I know her face. I knew it across ice, across a gallery, across the altar.

People imagine art is a mirror. They are lazy. Art is not reflection. Art is will. A canvas is a locked room where only the right shape is admitted. Isobel taught me that. Or I taught her. The order hardly matters now.

Some nights the memory arrives like a well-behaved child, hair smoothed and reciting the right words. Other nights it kicks the door. Today it slips in and stands by the window as if it has always been here. Isobel in the west wing, the room kept as the house kept its own organs. I had closed the door on visitors until the hinges learned the lesson. Father understood the need for quiet when I explained it properly. Men will always understand a lesson if it preserves their pride. I hung a thick cloth at the transom to press down the sound of the piano in the hall. She liked to look at it even when she could not play, the lid closed like a casket. I arranged the bottles on the nightstand in the order she would accept them. Bitter, then sweet, then nothing. It is important to create the right procession. Ritual teaches the body its fate.

She slept. Or performed sleep for me. She was very good at performance. That is why she belongs to me even now. Sometimes she would open her eyes without moving her head and watch me from that small slice of sight while I mixed paint by the window. The snow threw gray light into the room and her face returned it. She would ask for water. I would give it sparingly because mercy is a poor diet. Some days she would obey me and keep it down, some days she would disobey even that small kindness. It is not the role of the son to be endlessly forgiving. A son is a kind of priest. He keeps the ritual on course.

The doctors were an interruption, an insult. White coats always mistake interference for care. They wanted to drag her into bright rooms and boil her away with their lights. I closed that door. We had chosen a purer path and did not require their commerce.

She told me once, in the slow voice she used when she was remembering being a girl, that she wanted to be seen exactly as she was. Not medicated into courtesy, not flattered into a lie. Seen. That is what I gave her, more faithfully than anyone. The tissues beneath thinning skin. The mouth unpainted by powder but painted by me. The eyes that learned, at last, how to be still. People call decline cruel because they fear accuracy. It is not cruel to record the truth if the truth is beautiful.

Father raged at doors and you could hear it travel through the house like weather, but he did not rage in that room. He never learned the language of thresholds. He announced himself to wood and wood answered him with splinters. He was a minor god of noise. He died of himself. I kept Mother alive long enough to be perfect.

When I lifted my brush in those last weeks, I knew precisely what I was building. Immortality is not a fairytale. It is a technique. You give the body to silence and the face to oil. You keep the light where you want it and all the ugly, needy air where it belongs, outside, beyond the door. She asked me, once, if I forgave her for what she was denying me by leaving. I told her there is nothing to forgive when a person does their work. Her work was to be eternal. Mine was to make it true. She wept like a saint, quietly.

People talk about the dead as if they are victims of physics. They are merely victims of poor planning. No one speaks that way about my mother because I have not permitted it. The house remembered her properly because I taught it how.

Ellen misunderstood. She put her hands where they did not belong and called curiosity a virtue. She touched the box in the Blue Suite. She opened a door that wasn't hers and flinched at the air inside as if grief were a contagion. She had talent for sorrow, and that is why I chose her, but she had not yet learned reverence. She behaved as if life were the only altar that counted. I have always preferred winter altars.

The city outside my window is busy making a temporary religion of green. It paints its cheeks and drinks its declarations and then breaks them in the morning. Boston is a child you both indulge and correct. The noise is pleasant. It keeps most men from hearing what matters. But I hear very well. I heard the ice crack before she did. The lake is not unkind, it is just old and bored. It gave me a lesson and waited to see if I would repeat it properly. When it took me down, it did not take me by surprise. Cold taught me long ago how to turn the body into a machine. You save heat for the parts that sign your name on the world. The skin is a suit. The heart is the only document anyone reads.

People will tell you the sudden cold makes the chest lock, that the breath goes stingy and the limbs forget their purpose. That is true for men who never learned how to arrange themselves. I have always been good at arrangement. You do not panic, you just count. You do not thrash, you aim. There was a seam in the ice and I moved under it. A darker stripe where tide and wind conspired to make a thinner skin. I put my hands where the lake was least sure of itself and it allowed me to return. The air above felt like fire in my lungs. The shore of the world came back into shape. I lay under an alder root and listened to the house wonder aloud where I had gone.

It is not difficult to vanish if you remember that most people prefer stories to facts. The deputy at the boathouse had a face that would have pleased a medieval painter, plain, decent, a landscape of beginnings and ends. Men like that see what they expect to see and feel righteous about it. A borrowed coat, a different hat, a walk that says I am not the man you are hunting, and the world obliges. Winter helps because everyone is covered, and everyone is some version of the same animal. The road takes you if you know how to speak its language. The city opened for me. Cities love a man with a plan.

I found these rooms because they are modest and because they have the only view that matters. The landlord wanted a story about a job, so I gave him the truth. I am a painter. He liked the romance of that and not the smell, but I pay him in cash that has a respectful crispness, and romance humors even practical men when it is tidy. The stairwell coughs heat. The hall smells like fried onions and a wet dog that refuses to be housebroken. All of it is virtue in the proper measure because all of it makes me uninteresting.

The window is a frame. I hang my day in it. It looks across a narrow street into another rectangle of life. The building faces mine like a second canvas on the easel, waiting for the first stroke. Her rooms are small, and she has made them behave. She believes in baskets for toys and hooks for coats and a dish near the door where keys learn to stay. She sets her coffee near the stove, where the heat is most courageous, and sells her mornings to words with her hair tied back. She is teaching the city her shape. The city is grateful. It prefers women who do not require tending. It does not know, yet, how easily such women slip into worship when they meet someone who can finally see.

She has not bothered to pull the blinds today. She thinks safety is out there with the city's noise. Watching is a form of blessing in any serious theology. I stand a little to one side so the glass does not tattletale my interest back at her. Ellen is at the table with the small one, the doll hugged face-out like an icon. The eldest stalks the room with a book as if she can fence life with paper. I feel a tenderness toward that ferocity. It will eventually burn out if handled properly. Sparks become ash, and ash is very obedient to the slightest breath.

I have not yet decided which moment to paint as the center of her eternity. The ice is obvious, and I rarely forgive obviousness. The Blue Suite would be cleaner, but the room belongs to another narrative and I do not like thematic theft. Perhaps this is the new perfection, I at my easel, she framed in her own window. A diptych of devotion. I will need to soften the city's edges. Boston's bricks have the wrong vocabulary for reverence. But it can be taught. Everything can.

I remember the first time I watched Mother sleep without trying to make her comfortable. The light came in along the floor and climbed her body like an argument. Her breath had the courtesy to take shallow bows and then leave. I waited for panic and it did not arrive. But clarity did. We had finished something, she and I. I painted quickly because true things should not have to pose for long. Father banged at other doors. I did not let him in. He was a loud man, so he did not deserve a quiet room. Later, when the house learned grief's new language and everyone was allowed to talk in it, they wanted to make her death a scandal. It is the reflex of small people to make what they do not understand into a weapon. I walked through the rooms and turned all the portraits to face the wall for a day and the house understood who its priest was. It has obeyed me since.

If I close my eyes, I can lay out the next months like a good composition. Spring will come with its vulgar enthusiasms. The lake will loosen its jaw and belch out what it can no longer be bothered to keep. Men will poke at water with poles and congratulate themselves on their industry. They will talk about recovery and closure the way people talk about pie. Or they will find nothing and make a monument to nothing. Ellen will be told one version or the other, and either way she will feel the same shiver that I am near. It is not cruelty to give your subject a sense of scale. Fear increases the size of what love must fill. She will love better if she is afraid. She will be truer if she understands the frame.

I am not in a hurry. Time fattens art. Ripeness requires

neglect. I will watch her mornings get braver and her nights make bargains. I will learn the weather of her faces, the brief cloud when she thinks of the Adirondacks and of the diary and of the room that kept its perfume like a stubborn lie. She will dress the girls for school. She will tuck them into small beds. She will look at the door twice before she locks it. She will check the windows. She will take comfort in the noise outside and cry when the city finally sleeps and the small sound in her chest she calls a heart asks an unpleasant question. What would it be like to surrender to me, rather than fight? She will not like the word surrender. She will try other, nicer ones. Devotion, maybe. Safety. Permanence. She has always wanted to belong to something larger than bills. Bills are not churches. But I am.

She moves closer to the window now, drawn by the parade's noise. Green hats pass below, drums quick as a frightened pulse line the curb, a man in a foam shamrock wobbles by with a dignity I almost admire. Ellen laughs at something the small one says, and I am briefly angry with the city for thinking it can make her laugh without my permission. Then I remember permission and laughter are both mine to collect later, like canvases that need a final glaze.

I clean my thumb, then press it lightly into the wet paint at Ellen's temple on the canvas and leave a tiny crescent. A signature no one else will notice. I like to keep a piece of myself where a viewer thinks the subject is entire.

Across the way, she leans down to say something to the girls. The small one lifts her arms to be held. The elder one pretends she is beyond such bargains and then, predictably, slides closer under the excuse of reaching for a book. Ellen gathers them without asking their permission. She is better than she knows.

I feel it then, the particular quiet that means a room and I agree. I go to the window and fit myself to one side of it, so there is no profile in glass, no silhouette for the street. I place my hand on the frame. It is warm from radiators and sun. She lifts her face. For a half-breath I think she looks straight at me, and I have to put my other hand on the glass to steady the moment. But she looks through me, of course. She always has, since we've been framed in these windows.

I know what the next breath of her life will taste like. She will answer a phone. A voice will tell her a story about lakes and failure. Her mouth will close on the shape of his name, my name, but she will not say it. She will tell the girls they are staying in. She will draw the curtains and try not to blush when she realizes she is still afraid of windows.

I can wait. Waiting is a husband's discipline and a son's pleasure. The city will teach her how to call what is coming inevitability. I will teach her how to call it love.

I sit back on the stool and pick up my brush. I load it with a thin wash of green. Not the parade's liars' green, not the cheap paint of hats, but the green under skin that appears in good light when a person holds their breath and imagines jumping. I lay it down along the edge of her jaw on the canvas and then lift my eyes again.

Across the narrow street, Ellen stands in her window, talking to the girls. She believes glass is a wall. From here, it is merely a frame.

Printed in Dunstable, United Kingdom

70700793R00129